Christmas in Featherlow Bottom

PATRINA McKENNA

Copyright © 2021 Patrina McKenna

All rights reserved

This book is a work of fiction. Names, characters, places, and incidents either are products of the author's imagination or are used fictitiously. Any resemblance to actual persons, living or dead, events, or locales is entirely coincidental.

Publisher: Patrina McKenna

patrina.mckenna@outlook.com

ISBN-13: 978-1-8381827-2-4

Also by Patrina McKenna

Romantic comedy with a twist!

Truelove Hills
Truelove Hills – Mystery at Pebble Cove
Truelove Hills – The Matchmaker
Granny Prue's Bucket List
Christmas with the Neighbours
Trouble at Featherlow Forbes Menswear
Lady Featherlow's Tea Room
Christmas in Featherlow Bottom

Feel good fantasy for all the family!

GIANT Gemstones
A Galaxy of Gemstones
The Gemstone Dynasty
Enrico's Journey
Summer Camp at Tadgers Blaney Manor

DEDICATION

For my family and friends

1

FIRST NIGHT NERVES

The customers in the tea room were all ears. The much-awaited pantomime at Featherlow Bottom's Woodside Theatre opened last night and, Fifi, the tea room manager, had been one of the lucky ones to get a ticket.

Bella sat forward in her chair. 'Oh, do tell us all about it, Fifi. Ted and I won't be going until later in the week. Lucy went straight to bed when she got home after the performance. She was in such a strop – you'd think she was in her teens, not her thirties.'

Fifi wiped her hands on her apron. 'It was OK. You know what it's like – first night nerves and everything.'

Bella sighed. 'I thought it was a mistake to give all

the little ones in the village the chance to play a part. They always say, "never work with children or animals".'

Sam sat at a table next to the window eating his daily doughnut. He'd been deep in thought since his wife, Eleanor, had returned home last night in an agitated state. Eleanor was Head of Amateur Dramatics in the village, and casting for Prince Charming had been a nightmare. From her account, Ivan from the pub had fluffed his lines on several occasions, and Ted and Bella's daughter, Lucy, was threatening to resign as Cinderella.

Fifi glanced out of the tea room window to the sight of Ivan walking along the embankment with his shoulders slumped and his hands thrust into pockets. He was walking towards Archie's Alehouse on his way to do his day job. Her heart went out to him. Some people just weren't cut out for acting.

*

Eleanor climbed the steps to Featherlow Manor. Giles, the butler, opened the door. 'Do you have an appointment? I haven't been advised of any visitors today.'

Eleanor patted Giles's arm. 'Oh, just let me in, Giles. I need to see Lady Featherlow urgently.' Eleanor reached into her handbag. 'I don't believe you bought a ticket to the pantomime. Here's one for tonight's performance.'

Giles frowned. 'But I'm on duty tonight.'

Eleanor smiled. 'You won't be needed tonight. Trust me. Just let Lady Featherlow know I'm here, then everything will fall into place.'

*

Lady Annabelle Featherlow practically skipped into the drawing room, much to the surprise of her husband. 'Winston! You'll never guess what's happened.'

Lord Featherlow peered over the top of his newspaper. 'Go on. Tell me.'

'It's a real Cinderella story. Ivan's had the sack; Lucy's resigned, and I've agreed with Eleanor it won't harm for us to manage without Ellie for the next three weeks.'

Winston folded the newspaper and placed it on the floor. 'You're talking in riddles, Annabelle. Enlighten me.'

Annabelle wrung her hands together as she grinned from ear to ear. 'Cinderella worked in the kitchen, and Ellie works in our kitchen. Ellie's the understudy for Lucy, and now that Lucy's resigned, the limelight's shining on Ellie.'

Winston rubbed his chin. 'Ellie doesn't just work in our kitchen – she runs it. She's a Michelin Star Chef. What about all the events we have on at the manor in the run-up to Christmas?' Winston loosened his collar. 'And, what about Christmas and New Year? Haven't you thought about that? The pantomime doesn't end until the 2nd of January.'

Annabelle sighed. 'Oh, don't be an old Scrooge. We can manage. I've already telephoned the Alehouse, and Francesca has offered to help out. Don't forget she used to work in the kitchen here before she married Archie. She's an obvious temporary replacement. We can't let Ellie miss the chance of being Cinderella. With all the publicity, she may even find her real Prince Charming.'

Winston raised his eyes to the ceiling. 'From what you've just told me, Prince Charming has been released from his role.'

Annabelle tapped her nose with her forefinger. 'Eleanor advises me that Prince Charmings from outside of the village are in abundance. She's got three lined up already. If there's one thing you can say about Eleanor, she's got lots of contacts, and she always gets the job done.' Annabelle turned and headed towards the door. 'I'm so pleased you agree to this, Winston. Eleanor's in the kitchen now breaking the news to Ellie. She's a real Fairy Godmother! Oh, and she had the good sense to advise me that we should give Giles a night off. The poor man couldn't get a ticket to the pantomime – they've been so scarce. Eleanor has a spare one for tonight. He'll be thrilled to see Ellie on the stage. It will be a whole new experience for him.'

*

With breakfast finished, Ellie had time to spare before the lunch preparations. She was surprised but pleased to see Eleanor. 'How did the show go last night? There was a dinner party for twenty here, so I was kept quite busy. I felt like Cinderella with all my friends at the theatre on Opening Night.' Twenty-nine-year-old Ellie chuckled as she reached for a kettle. 'Would you like a cup of tea?'

Eleanor sat down at the long wooden table and crossed her fingers beneath it. The village theatre scene was a far cry from her days treading the boards in London. The understudy for Cinderella would have been in the wings at every performance. The Woodside Theatre, although very dear to her heart, was just a low budget operation. She shook her head. 'There's no time for tea dear, there's no time to waste. You must come with me now. You're on stage in the leading role at seven o'clock tonight. Thank goodness we don't have a matinée today. I need you to bond with Prince Charming this afternoon – I do so hope there's chemistry.'

It was Ellie's turn to sit down at the table; she leant

across it. 'Is Lucy unwell? This can't be happening. I'm too busy here to work in the theatre. I only trained as an understudy to make new friends – I never thought I would be called upon for real!'

Eleanor reached across to hold the young woman's hand. 'You have nothing to worry about; I have cleared it all with Lady Featherlow. You are free to work with me for the next three weeks. Ivan was sacked; Lucy resigned, and I have a selection of professional Prince Charmings from London who are all keen to do me a favour.' Eleanor coughed. 'Unfortunately, I can't find one who can make the whole three weeks, so I have left it between them to agree who can do when, and one of them will be here by two o'clock this afternoon. They've assured me they won't let me down.'

Ellie's practical mind was on overdrive. 'Well, I'll need to leave instructions for today's lunch and dinner, then we'd best go. Lucy's much taller and slimmer than me; the costumes will need altering. Will these new actors know the lines?'

Eleanor stood up and brushed down her skirt. 'The wardrobe team are waiting for us. And, yes, they all know the lines. What budding young actor doesn't want to be Prince Charming?'

2

ALL CHANGE

It was a hive of activity back at the theatre. Eleanor strode across the room to establish whose bag was "ringing" before discovering it was hers. She pulled out her phone.

'Am I speaking to Eleanor Dorrit?'

Eleanor left Ellie with the seamstress and walked into the corridor to take the call. 'Yes. Eleanor Dorrit speaking.'

'My name's Henry Spinnaker from The National Performing Arts Chronicle. I'm sure you've heard of us.'

Eleanor fluffed up her hair. 'Oh, Mr Spinnaker, I'm an absolute fan! I subscribe annually. What can I do for you?'

'Well, it's a bit of a long shot, but I wondered if I could pop along to your theatre tonight. Don't worry; I won't be doing a review. It's purely a pleasure visit. I'm stranded in the next village until tomorrow; my car's broken down.' There was silence down the line. 'Are you still there, Eleanor?'

'Yes . . . yes, I'm here.'

'I was at a loss with what to do this evening – until I saw the notice for your pantomime in the hotel reception area. How lucky was that? It sounds just the ticket!'

Eleanor's nerves were on edge, and she snapped, 'We don't have any tickets.' This was the last thing they needed with the changes taking place tonight. However, it wasn't good to be rude to a member of the press. She took a deep breath before continuing, 'But there's always room for a VIP. Just come along for six-forty-five, and I'll leave instructions for you to be seated.'

Henry smiled with satisfaction. 'Jolly good! That all sounds splendid.'

Eleanor pushed her phone to the bottom of her bag. She decided not to advise the cast an employee of The National Performing Arts Chronicle would be in the audience tonight. It wasn't a big deal – Henry Spinnaker was only on a social visit.

With the alterations underway for Ellie's costumes, there was time for a quick bite to eat before the first Prince Charming arrived. Ellie decided to pop over to Archie's Alehouse.

'Ivan! I'm so sorry to hear what happened last night. Have you heard that Lucy resigned after you left, and now I'm chained to the role of Cinderella for the next three weeks?'

There was a twinkle in Ivan's grey eyes, and as he nodded, his thick brown fringe flopped across his face. He brushed it away before speaking, 'I'm fully informed, Ellie. I must admit it's a huge relief. I should never have let Lucy persuade me to take on the role in the first place.'

Ellie smiled. 'That's great. I'm pleased you're OK. I'm shocked Lucy resigned, though. She was perfect for the role.'

Ivan leant forward on the bar and lowered his voice. 'Between you and me, she thought the pantomime would fold without her. She told me you weren't good enough to replace her, and there wasn't anyone to replace me, so she was off before word of last night's disaster got to the press.' Ivan snorted. 'The press, I ask you! When did the press ever reach the dizzying heights of Featherlow Bottom?'

Ellie held her shoulders back. 'Well, Lucy was wrong. I am more than capable of being Cinderella, and Eleanor has Prince Charmings queuing up to work with me.' Ellie climbed onto a bar stool. 'Talking of which, I need a quick tuna mayonnaise sandwich and an orange juice before I meet the first one.'

*

Back at the theatre, Prince Charming had arrived – his name was Luke. Eleanor fluttered around him like a mother hen. 'Good height, nice teeth, great eye contact. You certainly fit the bill, Luke. How long will you be with us?'

Luke ran a hand through his curly blonde hair. 'Just a week. Marcus will take over until Christmas Eve, and Antonio will be here from Boxing Day until the 2nd of January.'

Eleanor let out a sigh of relief. 'You boys have saved my life!'

Luke turned his attention to Ellie; she was dressed in a pale blue ballgown with a seamstress lying on the floor pinning up the hemline. Ellie held her hands in the air. 'I'm five-foot-five. The previous Cinderella was over six-foot in heels. I'm causing everyone a shocking amount of work.' Ellie held out her hand to shake Luke's. 'Nice to meet you, by the way.'

Luke took hold of Ellie's hand and kissed it. She was just what he liked; a leading lady much shorter than him. He'd easily be able to swing her around the stage in the ballroom scene. She wasn't bad looking either. She wore her chestnut hair tied up in a ponytail, but Luke guessed it would fall below her shoulders when loose, and her blue eyes were clear and sparkling.

'It's a pleasure to meet you too, Ellie. Shall we run through some lines whilst your alterations are being carried out?'

Ellie frowned. 'I thought you knew the lines.'

Luke laughed. 'Of course, I know the lines; it would just be good to go through them together. Perhaps when we've done that, you could show me to Archie's Alehouse – I'm booked in there for the week. We could have a drink before the show.'

Ellie raised her eyebrows. 'I'm happy to show you where your accommodation is, but I won't be drinking before the show.'

Luke grinned. 'I'll buy you a drink after then to celebrate.'

'What will we be celebrating?'

'The best first-night performance of a pantomime in Featherlow Bottom.'

'But first-night was last night.'

'From what I hear, that was just a disastrous trial run. Tonight's the night, Ellie. You *shall* go to the ball. Get ready to shine.'

Eleanor slapped a hand to her chest. How wonderful! There was chemistry between Prince Charming and Cinderella. Suddenly her fears about the appearance of Henry Spinnaker seemed grossly unfounded.

3

TAKE TWO

Giles arrived at the theatre and took his seat in the front row of the Stalls. It was unfortunate the front row seats were a bit too near the stage; there had been complaints in the past about stiff necks and viewing distraction by being able to see into the wings. To enhance the experience for paying members of the audience, Eleanor kept the front row free for any last-minute hiccups that may occur. Having to bribe Giles with a ticket to get into Featherlow Manor was the first hiccup for tonight – the second one had been the surprise visit by Henry Spinnaker.

With ten minutes to "curtain up", Henry was shown to his seat next to Giles. He held out his hand to shake the butler's. 'My name's Henry. It's good to meet you. It looks like we're the only two in the front row.'

Giles shook the man's hand. 'I'm Giles. Yes – I'm surprised there are spare seats; I thought the pantomime was sold out.'

Henry sat down in his chair and held his head back to see up onto the stage. 'My guess is the front row is less than popular. There's not a good view from here.'

Giles offered Henry a mint imperial. 'Well, *I'm* not complaining. I'm pleased to have the chance to see Ellie perform. She's like a daughter to me.'

Henry sucked on the mint. 'A daughter? Do tell me how you became acquainted.'

'Oh, we work together at Featherlow Manor. I'm the butler, and Ellie works in the kitchen. Her name's Miss Ellie Floris to be precise, and she's a Michelin Star Chef.'

Henry placed his elbows on the arms of his chair and clasped his hands together over his ample stomach. 'How intriguing. Tell me more.'

'Well, it's a real Cinderella story. The pantomime opened last night, and Prince Charming got the sack. Cinderella resigned, and Ellie's been drafted in to take on the leading role.' Giles offered Henry another mint which he accepted before reaching into his pocket for a small notepad and pen. Giles was appreciative of the removal of Henry's arm, which had been invading his space. He kept *his* arms well within the boundary of his seat.

With the sound and lighting teams creating an expectancy amongst the audience, the curtain lifted to the sight of Cinderella sweeping the kitchen floor. Giles and Henry noticed Eleanor in the wings giving a thumbs-up sign. Ellie twirled around with the broom before the ugly sisters arrived to advise she hadn't been invited to the ball at the palace.

A scurrying in the wings caught the attention of the front row guests. Six children soon emerged from each side, brandishing fluorescent plastic swords to scare the ugly sisters away. They wore eye patches and striped t-shirts. Henry grabbed Giles's arm. 'This *is* Cinderella, isn't it? It looks more like Peter Pan.'

Giles pulled his arm free. 'It's definitely Cinderella. Eleanor's been very creative. How else was she going to give all the youngsters in the village an opportunity to be on the stage?'

Henry suppressed a chuckle. 'Well, I've never seen anything like *this* before.'

By the last scene before the interval, the mint imperials were all gone. Henry's notepad lay open on the seat next to him, and his mouth was ajar at the sight of Cinderella outside a castle calling up to a tower: 'O Romeo, Romeo, wherefore art thou Romeo?' He wiped a tear from his eye.

'Well, I never. There's a bit of Shakespeare in here too. What's Romeo got to do with it?'

Giles tutted. 'You need to concentrate. Romeo is Cinderella's ex-boyfriend. Prince Charming is going to have a difficult time winning her over. Be quiet now; it's getting to a good bit.'

*

Luke paced around his dressing room. He'd never performed in such a shambles of a show before. He'd only had a minor part to play in the first half but, after the interval, Prince Charming was in every scene. He needed a drink. If the clock on the wall was correct, there were five minutes until the intermission. He pulled on his jeans and jumper and headed for the bar.

*

As the curtain fell, Henry rose to his feet. 'Let's go to the bar, Giles. I owe you a drink after eating all your mints.'

Giles remained seated. 'I'm fine here, Henry. I'll make do with an ice cream.'

Henry headed towards the Exit. 'You wait there

then. I'll bring a couple of ice creams back.'

*

Luke was drinking his gin and tonic when Henry appeared down the other end of the bar and ordered one for himself. Luke's eyes were on stalks. What was Henry Spinnaker doing here? That man had ruined many an actor's reputation; how devious of Eleanor to hide his presence from the cast. Luke went in search of Ellie. He knocked on her dressing room door.

'Come in.'

'Ellie! I have the worst news. Henry Spinnaker is in the audience.'

'Henry who?'

Luke sighed. The name obviously wasn't important in the amateur dramatics community. 'It's nothing for you to worry about, but my career will be on the line if I fluff my lines tonight.'

'You said you knew the lines.'

'Well, yes and no. I've never been in a pantomime like this before.'

'You haven't?'

'No! It's . . . well, it's a bit of a mixture.' Ellie's eyes widened, and Luke knelt before her. He took hold of her hands. 'I need you to trust me and just go with the flow in the second half. I'm going to have to ad-lib quite a bit.'

'Ad-lib! Why?'

'Just to make the performance more authentic.'

'If you're "ad-libbing" then what am I going to do?'

'Just be Cinderella. Take my lead and say what comes into your head. Pretend you're in love with me. Can you do that?'

Ellie blushed. There was more chance of her being able to pretend with Luke than there ever was with Ivan. 'I'll do my best.' The bar-bell rang with a five-minute warning for the audience to return to their seats. Ellie stood up. 'But, if we both get the sack after tonight, then don't blame me.'

*

Eleanor was on tenterhooks. The second half of the show wasn't going to plan. For one thing, she didn't recognise most of the lines. She dragged a chair into the wings and sat with her head in her hands. What was Luke playing at? The ugly sisters and the children were all conforming; even the Fairy Godmother was sticking rigidly to the script. It was just Luke, and shockingly Ellie, who had chosen to throw caution to the wind and do their own thing.

Eleanor peered between her fingers at Henry Spinnaker in the front row of the audience. She soon realised he could see her too. He was roaring with laughter one minute and crying the next – this was a total disaster! Eleanor stood up, grabbed her chair, and edged her way backstage.

With the standard Cinderella scenes out of the way, the finale was scripted to enhance the story. The stage was set for a wedding reception.

Henry nudged Giles. 'That's an extra bit; I wonder what they'll do here.'

This was the part where Eleanor's heart was in her mouth. She'd bribed all the children to be "good" wedding guests with the offer of lollipops when they came off the stage. Her words to them every night before this scene were: 'Be seen, but not heard.'

With the cast and children all seated at trestle tables, Prince Charming and his bride took centre stage. This was the time for them to take their bows and any applause the audience chose to offer . . . but not tonight. Luke turned around and took hold of a cupcake before squashing it on top of a pirate's head. There were gasps throughout the cast and audience, and Eleanor's knees buckled beneath her. She staggered towards her chair. Luke winked at the sound manager, and a rendition of "Dancing Queen" blasted through the speakers. He twirled Ellie around as the pirates took it upon themselves to climb onto the tables for a real bun fight.

Ellie couldn't contain her laughter. 'What on earth are you doing? We are going to be in soooo much trouble!'

Luke held her tightly. 'I don't care.'

Henry blew his nose. 'I don't believe it! Cinderella finishing off with a touch of Mamma Mia! Now I've seen everything.'

Eleanor had fainted. A wardrobe mistress knelt on the floor next to her with a bottle of smelling salts . . . it was a shame she missed the standing ovation.

4

POST SHOW REVIEW

The following morning, Luke and Ellie sat opposite Eleanor holding hands. Luke spoke first: 'We're very sorry for mixing things up a bit and changing the lines, but I have previous experience of Henry Spinnaker and know what it takes to push his buttons. By the way, it was a bit naughty of you not to mention he was in the audience. It was lucky I caught sight of him at the bar during the interval.'

Eleanor knew she should be annoyed with Luke, but he had such a charming way about him it was hard to be cross for long. She was determined, though, not to let him get away lightly with hijacking her show. 'Firstly, Henry Spinnaker was here on a social visit; he won't be doing a review. Secondly, why were you at the bar during the interval of last night's performance?'

Luke lowered his eyes. 'I needed a drink . . . just a soft one.'

Eleanor made a note on the pad in front of her. 'I'll arrange for a carafe of water to be available in your dressing room for future performances.'

Luke squeezed Ellie's hand. 'Does that mean I've not been sacked?'

Eleanor sat back in her chair and sighed. 'I know what actors are like; I was one, remember? Temperamental the lot of them. At the end of the day, if the audience is happy, then that's all that counts. I was worried we'd have to cancel the show after night one – there were requests for refunds. This morning the booking office is inundated with requests for tickets, and we're already sold out.'

Ellie was bubbling over with excitement. Luke hadn't let go of her hand yet, and her feet hadn't touched the ground since last night. 'Why don't we extend the show for another week?'

Eleanor shook her head. 'There's not much point in that. Luke's only here for the next six days. We can keep the changes to the scene at the end, but I doubt Marcus and Antonio will be so popular in the role. Luke shone like a Broadway star last night.'

Ellie turned to Luke, her blue eyes pleading. 'Can't you stay for the whole three weeks?'

Luke shook his head. 'Sorry. I'm off to Biarritz for Christmas. Besides, I don't think Eleanor's being fair to Marcus and Antonio – they each have their own qualities.' Luke released Ellie's hand and focused his gaze on Eleanor. 'Also, don't be surprised when tomorrow's edition of The National Performing Arts Chronicle has a write-up of last night's performance. I saw Henry Spinnaker's camera flash a few times. We could end up on the front page.'

*

Sure enough, Henry Spinnaker had written a review. It made page five of the Chronicle. Eleanor cut around the article carefully – this one would go in a frame. Her phone rang and she placed the scissors on a table before answering.

'Good afternoon, Eleanor Dorrit speaking.'

'Why, hello Eleanor. Henry Spinnaker here. I'm just calling to thank you for your hospitality the other evening. I'm also in need of another favour.'

'Oh, Henry! It's so good to speak to you; I've just seen your review of the show. You were very kind.'

'That's not normally a word associated with me. I tell things straight. I must admit I haven't laughed so much in a long time. I enjoyed the company of Giles the butler too. He's a mine of information. It's due to Giles that I'm coming back to Featherlow Bottom next week.'

Eleanor raised her eyebrows. 'Is that so?'

'It certainly is. Next time I'll be bringing my son, Beau, with me.'

'Really, that's nice.'

Henry continued, 'Giles informed me the Headquarters of Featherlow Forbes Menswear has moved from London to Featherlow Bottom. I've known Lord Winston Featherlow for years. Now he's retired, I'm keen to become acquainted with his son, Freddie.'

'Oh, that *is* nice.'

'Anyway, the reason for the call is to ask if you have any seats available for Monday night's performance. Beau and I are being measured up for new suits, and we're staying overnight. It's always good to spruce up a bit for Christmas.'

Eleanor checked her diary. 'Monday the 20th of December. Let me see . . . I could fit you in the front row again.'

Henry wasn't surprised. Still, a cricked neck was worth it. Beau would be in fits of giggles for most of the show. 'Great! We'll be staying in the village this time. Giles has recommended Archie's Alehouse for accommodation. We'll see you on Monday!'

Eleanor dropped her phone into her bag then slapped a hand to her forehead; Monday was Marcus's first night. This pantomime was taking years off her life! Why was everything so complicated?

*

At Featherlow Manor, Lord Featherlow sat in the drawing room with his son. 'You're doing a great job, Freddie. I didn't once think about moving the Headquarters closer to home when I commuted to London for all those years. From what I've seen and heard, all seems to be working tickety-boo.'

Freddie sat forward in his chair and handed his father a copy of the latest Management Accounts. 'The figures are up. Even with the cost of the new showroom and offices here in the village. We've released some of the London office space now, so that's brought a huge saving.'

Winston nodded approvingly as he surveyed the figures. 'I almost forgot to mention, an old friend of mine is coming down next week – Henry Spinnaker. He's been a customer of ours for years. Henry owns a publication to do with the theatre. He'll be bringing his son with him on Monday – they both need suit fittings.'

Freddie's deep blue eyes shone from the light of the roaring fire. Giles walked in with a tray of drinks without shutting the door, and Freddie stood up to warm his hands. 'Well, I hope the weather holds out for them. Snow's forecast. Thankfully, we're not going far before Christmas. I'm quite looking forward to a small family gathering with just you, Mother, Amelie and me.'

Winston raised his eyes to the ceiling. 'Well, we've had to cut back on entertaining this year with Ellie leaving us in the lurch.'

Freddie chuckled. 'I hear Ellie's doing very well as Cinderella. You could say she's saved the day. The Woodside Theatre will be getting quite a reputation. Maybe your friend could arrange for one of his colleagues to write a review for his publication.'

Giles poked his head back into the room and coughed. 'Mr Spinnaker's written a review himself, and it's glowing.' He then disappeared, closing the door behind him.

Freddie laughed. 'Who needs "flies on the wall" when we've got Giles.' He ran a hand through his shiny black hair before sitting down. 'Now, tell me all about the Spinnakers; I'll provide them with first-class service when they arrive. It's always good to keep on the right side of the press.'

5

CHEMISTRY LESSON

Ellie and Luke sat at a window table in Archie's Alehouse, reading the lunch menu. However, Ellie's mind was elsewhere. She looked over at Luke with his sparkling turquoise eyes, and her heart sank. 'What am I going to do without you? We've had standing ovations for all performances over the last five days. How am I going to be able to work with Marcus after that? We're not even following the script. I don't think I can even remember the original script.'

Luke smiled over the top of his menu. 'I think I'll have the lasagne. What do you fancy?'

Ellie sat back and folded her arms; infatuation was fast turning to annoyance. 'Luke! You're not listening to me. We've had such great chemistry that I don't know if I can continue as Cinderella without you.' Ellie regretted her words as soon as they were said. What had she turned into? She was a Michelin Star Chef, a hard woman, a career girl who was as tough as they came. Heaven knows she'd given up everything to follow her dream of getting to the top of her profession. Why on earth was she now whimpering about being at a loss without Luke?

Luke reached across the table to hold her hand. 'You'll have great chemistry with Marcus and Antonio too. If you've mastered it with me, you can do the same with anyone. You're a good actress, Ellie. I wish I were as multi-talented as you; I'm rubbish in the kitchen. Now, would you recommend the lasagne or not? I'll wait to see what you're having; then I may change my mind.'

After removing her hand from beneath Luke's, Ellie picked up the menu and hid behind it whilst she regained her composure. Luke was right; she was a good actress. She'd convinced everyone, including herself, that she wasn't interested in long-term relationships. Her job was far too important to allow a man into her life. She hadn't met any that came anywhere near making an effort for. Well, perhaps just the one, but he was just as committed to his job as she was to hers. Maybe now was the time to learn a bit about this "chemistry" thing.

Ellie placed the menu on the table. 'I'd recommend the lasagne. I'll have it too.'

Luke rubbed his hands together. 'Great!'

Ellie leant forward and spoke quietly. 'We've only got two days left before you disappear to Biarritz. Before you go you need to give me some lessons on chemistry; I'm a bit lacking in that area. It's been easy to get along with you, but you're a master of charm. Tell me what I need to do when you're gone.'

Luke rubbed his chin. 'How do you get along with Ivan? Any sign of chemistry there?'

Ellie shook her head. 'Definitely not!'

'Well, here's your first lesson. When Ivan comes over to take our orders, you need to catch his eyes with yours, blink a couple of times and brush his fingers when he takes your menu away. And smile. Always remember to smile.'

Before Ellie could complain, Ivan was standing next to their table. 'Have you decided what you'd like to eat?'

Luke handed his menu to Ivan. 'We certainly have. It's lasagne for the both of us.' Luke kicked Ellie under the table. She was holding onto her menu, and Ivan went to grab it. Ellie slipped her hand up the side of it and touched his fingers. Ivan stared at her in surprise, and she blinked a couple of times whilst smiling brightly. A redness crept up Ivan's neck onto his cheeks. Ellie had never paid any attention to him before. He mumbled, 'Right then, I'll get you some cutlery,' before heading off to the kitchen.

Ellie held her head in her hands. 'You are such a bad influence on me!'

Luke chuckled. 'It worked, though. You're in with a chance with him now if you're interested.'

Ivan returned with the cutlery and a small vase of flowers. He arranged the knives and forks on the table and placed the flowers in the centre. When Ivan turned, he caught Ellie's eye and winked. As soon as he was out of earshot, Ellie burst out laughing. 'The sooner you leave for your Christmas holidays, the better! You don't know the difference between chemistry and flirting. You've cheered me up, though. I'm woman enough to handle Marcus and Antonio. If I've managed to work with you, then I'll be able to work with anyone.'

Luke raised his glass of apple juice. 'You're making me jealous now. We need a toast: May all your Prince Charmings be good ones, but never as good as the first.'

The couple clinked glasses, and Ellie smiled. 'Let's just say you'll be a hard act to follow.'

*

Lucy was agitated. She was shocked and perturbed Ellie was surviving in the Cinderella role. Where on earth had Eleanor found another Prince Charming from? If Lucy had known Luke was waiting in the wings, she would never have resigned. It was most unfortunate that the curly-haired blonde was making women swoon. Even her mother was singing his praises after watching the pantomime last night.

Bella handed a copy of the programme to Lucy. 'It's a good job they didn't have photographs printed on these. They've only had to cross your name out and change it to Ellie's and scrub Ivan's out to make way for that nice young man's. There was a standing ovation at the end – it lasted for three whole minutes. Your father and I had a great time.'

Ted popped his head around the lounge door. 'You're missing a real treat, Lucy. I could see you with that new Prince Charming. He's a good height; you wouldn't have needed to bend down all the time. Still, there'll be other shows. Just make sure you don't jump ship too soon next time.'

Lucy threw the programme on the floor and marched out of the house. She'd been planning her revenge, and now was the time to take action. The Baker twins owed her a favour. She hadn't split on them when they'd cut six inches off an ugly sister's wig. That remained a mystery to the cast. Lucy grinned as she strode along the embankment towards the theatre; Billy and Bobby Baker would be the perfect partners in crime.

6

VIP CUSTOMERS

Freddie stood in the showroom of Featherlow Forbes Menswear, awaiting the arrival of Henry and Beau Spinnaker. He felt a great sense of satisfaction as he walked around the front salon, which contained this season's latest designs. The window dressers had surpassed themselves with a lavish Christmas display; they had also adorned the two arches dominating the plain brick back wall of the shop with foliage from the grounds of Featherlow Manor. The scent of pine filled the air, and as Freddie sipped the mulled wine that Charles, the showroom manager, had handed to him, he realised the old rogue had been heavy on the brandy again.

'Charles! There's too much brandy. You know I only gave you this job to keep you out of Archie's Alehouse.'

The older man let out a mighty chuckle. 'You'll always be young Freddie Featherlow to me. It wasn't too long ago that *I* had to keep *you* out of the pub.'

Freddie grinned, but not before putting his mulled wine down on a table. Hiring silver-haired Charles as the showroom manager had been a win-win situation for both of them. Although lacking in height, Charles was a giant amongst men with his wealth of knowledge and charming personality. He'd been a shining light in Featherlow Bottom until the death of his wife, Olivia, three years ago. Coaxing Charles out of retirement hadn't been easy but, if anyone could do it, it was Freddie.

Charles stood with hands on hips looking out of the window. 'The sky's darkening.' He then glanced at his watch. 'Twenty minutes before the snow comes. You mark my words.' Noticing Freddie's raised eyebrows, Charles continued, 'No need to worry. I've got whisky as well as brandy in the stockroom and a good selection of biscuits and board games.' Charles winked, and Freddie laughed, just as the door to the showroom opened to the sight of the Spinnakers unravelling their scarves.

'The weather's drawing in. It's a good job we're staying overnight. You must be Freddie Featherlow. I'm Henry Spinnaker, and this is my son Beau.' Henry blew into his hands before holding one out to shake Freddie's.

'I'm very pleased to meet you, Mr Spinnaker. My father has told me all about you.' Freddie shook Beau's hand too. 'I understand you're both here to be fitted for suits for Christmas. Our tailors are on standby and, once you've chosen the designs, we'll work around the clock to have them ready for you by tomorrow evening.'

Henry grinned. 'That's a pretty impressive turnaround. Can't say I've had the same service offered in London.'

Beau walked over to inspect a heather-grey lounge suit. 'I like this one. It looks my size.'

Henry shuffled his feet. 'Your mother won't be happy about you wearing that on Christmas Day. She's insisting on dinner suits.'

Beau smiled. 'I've got dinner suits I haven't even worn yet. Whilst we're here, it would be good to get something to wear for my new job.'

Charles appeared with a tray of mulled wine which Freddie hoped had been watered down. 'New job? Now, where might that be? I've just got a new job working here. There's nothing better than a new job. New job – new year. Where will you be off to for this new job?'

Freddie cringed. Charles wasn't usually so forward. When he was on the scent of something, though, he never gave up.

Henry answered on behalf of his son. 'Beau's not going far. He's taking up his new role in January. His mother and I couldn't be more proud.' Henry sipped a mulled wine as he headed towards one of the arches. 'My goodness! You have a whole wall in there devoted to Foxy Forbes! Now, she was a woman.' Henry walked through the arch, followed by Beau and Freddie.

Freddie was pleased to see the obvious delight on Henry Spinnaker's face. 'When we moved our Headquarters to Featherlow Bottom, I wanted to dedicate a room to the history of our business. We wouldn't be where we are today without Aunt Foxy. She was the co-founder along with my father – her brother – Lord Featherlow.'

Henry placed an arm around Freddie's shoulders. 'I know your family history, Son. Such a shame Foxy left us far too early. Still, I'm pleased to know old Winston is relying on you to keep the business in the family.' Henry glared at Beau. 'Nothing I admire more than a family business.'

Charles stood behind the counter at the entrance to the showroom and tapped away on a computer. He'd established that Henry Spinnaker was the owner of The National Performing Arts Chronicle and that he had three sons and a daughter. Beau was a chef; his short blonde hair and pale blue eyes were unmistakable. Charles scratched his head. Why would a chef need a lounge suit for his new job?

From the window, Charles noticed Billy and Bobby Baker heading towards the showroom. He jumped up and took two humbugs out of his pocket. Charles opened the door and held out his hand. 'I've no time to play today, boys. Take a sweet each instead. You can pop in again tomorrow, and we'll have another game of snakes and ladders.'

Bobby went red in the face. 'But we need to speak to you urgently.'

Charles shook his head. 'I have to go now. We can catch up tomorrow.' The boys turned around and headed off with their shoulders slumped. Charles noticed the first flakes of snow drifting down from the ever-darkening sky. His heart sank – the boys weren't wearing their gloves. How many times had he warned them snow was forecast today? His mood soon changed when he thought of the deepness of the snow by tomorrow. There was little chance he'd see the boys again before Christmas – they'd be out on their sledges. Charles grinned and headed off to make another round of mulled wine. Those Spinnakers might buy a couple of suits each if he loosened them up with a bit of Christmas spirit.

*

Freddie closed the door behind the VIP customers. What a result! Five suits between them, along with a watch, bracelet, and ring from the Featherlow Forbes Menswear jewellery collection. A team of tailors would be working through the night in the knowledge a job well done meant they could finish three days early for Christmas. If nothing else, the Featherlows were fair employers – all employees were looking forward to their annual hamper of produce from the Featherlow Manor estate.

'I'm grateful for your support today, Charles. I hope they're not too intoxicated on their way over to Archie's Alehouse. I wouldn't want to be fishing any customers out of the river.'

Charles laughed. 'I suggest you head off for the day now, Freddie. I'll call you if there's any need. The lane to the manor will blocked before long.'

Freddie nodded. 'You're right. I'm sure my father's on the case with the local farmer to have his snow plough on standby. Luckily, the Spinnakers are staying in the village tonight. They can walk to the theatre and back to the Alehouse; the roads should be clear tomorrow night for their journey home. I'll see you in the morning, Charles. Good work today!'

7

A NEW LEADING MAN

Ellie had spent the day with Marcus. It soon became apparent he wasn't as reckless as Luke – he was keen to stick rigidly to the lines. He was tall, with long red hair, which he wore in a "man bun" during rehearsals. His magnificent mane was complimented by piercing silver-grey eyes. He was, in fact, quite stunning.

Billy Baker hid a pair of scissors down one of his pirate boots, and Bobby shuffled a pocketful of marbles. Billy spoke first: 'Lucy said we have to do it tonight, or she'll tell our mum all our secrets.'

Bobby sighed. 'I don't want to do it. I like being in the pantomime. We'll be in more trouble than we're in already if we do what Lucy says.'

'But she said she's going to be watching us from the

wings.'

'I think it's a bit too much to ask of us – getting Cinderella to trip over on the marbles in the first scene. When are we supposed to cut a chunk out of Prince Charming's hair?'

'That's not until tomorrow. Lucy says Ellie will leave the show tonight as she'll have such a red face.'

'But why are we cutting Prince Charming's hair?'

'You need to keep up, Bobby. It's Lucy's backup plan. If Ellie doesn't resign so that Lucy can come back, we have to stop the whole show. We need to cut Prince Charming's hair whilst he's having a pre-show nap tomorrow afternoon.'

Bobby nodded. 'We'd best make a good job of the marbles, then. We'll be in less trouble if our first mission goes well.'

*

Henry and Beau Spinnaker took their seats in the front row of the Stalls, and Lucy paced around in the wings. She'd spoken to Eleanor that afternoon and offered her services as Ellie's understudy. All Lucy needed now was for the Baker twins to perform well in the first scene. Beau's attention was drawn to the gorgeous blonde as she strode back and forth. He nudged his father. 'Is that Cinderella in the wings? Surely she should be in costume by now.'

Henry leant forward to have a better look. 'No.

That's not Cinderella. Quite a beauty, isn't she? I don't remember seeing her last week. Maybe she's a wardrobe mistress.'

Beau's intrigue with the blonde was heightened; she was now wagging her finger at a little boy in a threatening manner. The child looked uncomfortable, and Beau stood up. 'I'm just popping to the bar for a quick one before the performance starts. Can I get you anything?'

Henry shook his head. 'Don't be long; the five-minute warning will sound soon.'

Beau didn't get to the bar; he was nearly knocked over by two little boys running towards him. They both wore striped shirts and looked identical. 'Whoa! What's the rush? Didn't I see one of you talking to a blonde lady a few minutes ago? Did she upset you?'

Bobby shook his head and wiped his face with his sleeve. 'It's nothing. It's just about a job.'

Beau smiled. 'What job?'

Billy stood with a straight back. 'My brother said it's nothing.'

Beau frowned. 'Who was the lady?'

Bobby felt the smoothness of the marbles in his pocket. 'Her name's Lucy. She used to be Cinderella, and now she wants her job back. Now, if you'll excuse us, we have things to do.'

Beau shrugged his shoulders. It was none of his business. The warning bell was sounding, and the bar had shut. What bad luck. He should have kept his nose out of things. This time tomorrow, he'd be on the train heading back to London for Christmas. It was such a pain his father had suggested this spur of the moment trip. He didn't even need a new suit.

Beau returned to his seat as the curtain was lifting. Cinderella was sweeping the floor, and Beau couldn't believe his eyes. Ellie! What was Ellie Floris doing on the stage? She was a Michelin Star Chef!

Henry whispered in his son's ear. 'What's up with you? You look like you've seen a ghost.'

Beau whispered back. 'I know that woman. She's not an actress; she's a chef.'

Henry winked. 'That's correct. It's a real Cinderella story. The original one resigned, and Ellie got plucked from the kitchen at Featherlow Manor to fill her shoes.' Henry chuckled. 'It's a good job they fit!'

Beau rubbed his chin. The blonde in the wings was still pacing around. What was she planning in order to get her job back? Whatever way, it involved those young boys. As if on cue, the boys appeared in the wings with several other children, and the former Cinderella was now demonstrating an underarm throwing action. The little boy from earlier nodded and reached into his trouser pocket to grab a handful of something. Ellie was spinning around on the stage with her broom as the boy released a handful of marbles!

Beau jumped up. 'Ellie! Watch your footing!'

There were gasps around the audience, and Beau climbed onto the stage. 'I'm sorry, ladies and gentlemen. From my position in the front row, I noticed a slippery patch on the stage. I'm sure it will be cleared quickly. Apologies for any inconvenience.'

The curtain dropped, and Ellie turned white. 'Beau! What are you doing here?'

'It's a small world, Ellie. I never thought I'd see you treading the boards.'

Ellie laughed. 'Neither did I!'

Billy and Bobby were crawling around on the floor collecting the stray marbles whilst Eleanor stood over them. Billy gave his best smile. 'We're so sorry. There was a hole in Bobby's pocket.'

Eleanor held her head in her hands. 'You're lucky there wasn't an accident. If you bring marbles into the theatre again, you will both be fired!'

Beau bent down to whisper to Ellie. 'Watch out for Lucy – she wants her job back.'

Ellie laughed. 'What? Why? She resigned.'

Beau held his hands in the air. 'I don't know the details. Just trust me.'

Beau bent down and kissed the top of Ellie's head.

'It would be great to have a catch-up with Cinderella after the show. I'll wait for you at the Stage Door.'

Ellie turned pink. 'There's no need for that. I've promised to go for an after-show meal with Marcus.'

'Who's Marcus?'

'The new Prince Charming. It's his first night tonight.'

'Oh, I see. Well, Father and I will be leaving tomorrow evening. Any chance of lunch before I head back to London?'

Ellie shook her head. 'I think it's best we leave things as they are. I'm done with complications.'

Beau nodded. 'I'm sorry for the way it turned out, Ellie. I've regretted it ever since.'

Ellie picked up her skirt before going in search of her broom. Beau Spinnaker was best to be avoided; the sooner he left Featherlow Bottom, the better. Her focus was back on the pantomime – and the new Prince Charming; he had such lovely eyes.

8

A FOILED PLAN

Lucy was angry, and she didn't know who to blame. Well, she did . . . it was a rather handsome stranger who had scuppered the marbles stunt. That very same man was at the bar now with an older gentleman who was waving to her.

'Do come and join us, my dear. I saw you looking over; you must recognise me from The National Performing Arts Chronicle.' Lucy edged nearer to the men and took hold of the hand extended to her. 'I'm Henry Spinnaker, and this is my son, Beau.'

As Lucy flashed a smile, her pale blue eyes bore into Beau with such animosity he took a step backwards. Lucy breathed in deeply; she had to regain her composure. 'I'm very pleased to meet you both. May I ask why you are in Featherlow Bottom on such a dismal night?'

Henry laughed. 'Dismal? The weather's a bit bleak, I agree. But the pantomime is delightful. I came last week and couldn't resist another fun night out whilst I'm in the village. Beau's enjoying himself as much as me. Cinderella is outstanding, and I can't wait to see more of the new Prince Charming. What part do you play in the production? Now, let me guess – wardrobe mistress.'

Lucy was about to explode. Who did these Spinnakers think they were? Apart from foiling the plan to bring Ellie to her knees from the dizzying heights of stardom, the older one had taken it upon himself to insult her. Beau tried to contain his smile as Lucy's pretty face flared up in red blotches.

Henry wasn't letting go. 'Go on. If it's not wardrobe mistress, then maybe you're in administration.' Henry's eyes were twinkling; he'd noticed the evil look the woman had given his son; he just couldn't work out why. 'I've got it! You work in the cloakroom. I think we saw you on the way in.'

Lucy's nails dug into the palms of her hands. She flashed another of her evil looks, this time at Henry Spinnaker, before turning and shouting over her shoulder. 'I'm the real Cinderella!'

Henry stared at Beau. 'Well, I never. The

pantomime in this theatre continues off the stage. She's a character, that one. It appears Cinderella's got more enemies than just a couple of ugly sisters and a wicked stepmother.'

Beau cringed; his father couldn't be more right.

*

Archie's Alehouse was the only place catering for after-show meals. They were popular with the cast. Henry and Beau had eaten before the pantomime and now sat up at the bar with brandies. Beau's eyes were locked on the table for two in the bay window. He couldn't hear what Ellie and Marcus were discussing, but there was a rapport between the two. Ellie was shrieking and covering her mouth with her hand. She reached into her pocket for a tissue to wipe her eyes. Beau was on red alert. Was Marcus upsetting her, or was he amusing her?

Ellie leant forward and grabbed Marcus's hand. 'I don't believe you! You've got to be joking.'

Marcus shook his head. 'I'm not. I'm serious – my hair is a wig. It's blonde underneath. I thought I'd spice things up after Luke's huge success last week. Two blonde Prince Charmings in a row would have been boring.'

Ellie chuckled. 'Boring? Who for?'

'You, of course.'

Ellie blushed and fanned herself with a menu. 'You're such a flirt.'

It was now Marcus's turn to laugh. 'Can you blame me? You're gorgeous. Luke's never been so smitten with a leading lady. He gave me a pretty hefty "hands-off" warning as far as you're concerned.'

Ellie frowned. 'Luke did what??'

'Luke told me to "cut the chemistry" as I'd be wasting my time. He said Antonio would be more your type – you go for Italian stallions.'

Ellie snorted. 'Italian stallions! Luke's making that up. I've always preferred blondes.' Ellie glanced up at the bar, and her heart missed a beat when Beau waved to her. Now, *he* was her type; it was a shame he valued his career more than a relationship.

Beau was hatching a plan. He needed to stay longer in Featherlow Bottom to protect Ellie and having his father around was a distraction. The weather was forecast to get worse from tomorrow lunchtime; it would be brilliant if he could get stranded in the village for a couple of days. He took a swig of brandy and tried his luck. 'The weather's going to get worse tomorrow, Father. I'm worried you won't get back in time for the Chronicle's Christmas Party. You've never missed one before. Why don't you get the train back to London tomorrow morning, and I'll stay on to collect the suits.'

Henry smiled. 'But you need to get back for the party too. I'm going to announce your new role in the family business.'

Beau shifted in his seat. 'I'll do everything I can to get back in time. But, if not, you can delay the announcement until the New Year.'

Henry frowned. 'I must admit I was worried we were cutting it a bit fine tomorrow. Are you sure you don't mind waiting around for the suits?'

Beau shook his head. 'It's no problem at all. I'll be back in London before you know it.'

Henry slapped his son on the back. 'You're going to be a real asset to the team, Beau.' Henry yawned before finishing his brandy. 'I don't know about you, Son, but I'm ready for bed.'

9

BACKUP PLAN

Charles turned on the small radio under the showroom counter; it kept him company when there were no customers around. This morning, it would be quiet, with thick snow covering the ground and another heavy fall forecast by lunchtime. The Spinnakers weren't due until four o'clock, so Charles set about dusting the shelves on the back wall.

> *It's Tuesday the 21st of December, and we have a great music mix planned for you today, starting with the Bing Crosby classic – White Christmas.*

Charles sang along in a deep voice; he was engrossed in his work until an icy breeze made him shudder. Charles turned to see the Baker twins standing in the open doorway. 'Goodness, you scared me! I wasn't expecting anyone this morning. Come in and shut the door behind you. It's freezing out there today. Are you here for that game of snakes and ladders?'

The boys shook their heads. Billy spoke first: 'We're in trouble, and we need your help.'

Charles stood with hands on hips. 'What is it this time?'

Bobby lowered his eyes. 'We don't have a turkey.'

Charles sighed. 'Oh, you poor children. Your mother can't afford a turkey this Christmas. That's terrible.'

Bobby was about to speak, and Billy elbowed him in the ribs. They had to get a turkey from somewhere, so their mother didn't find out they'd spent the deposit on sweets. It had taken them weeks to save up more money, and when they'd gone to the farm yesterday, the farmer advised them there were no turkeys left. All deposits had been paid in October, and the turkeys were now resting in the barn, ready for collection on Christmas Eve.

It had crossed Billy's mind they could sneak in the barn and grab a turkey, but he'd thought better of it. If they got caught this afternoon on their mission for

Lucy, then Christmas would be cancelled. Best not to get caught stealing a turkey too. Why was life so difficult?

The showroom door flew open to the sight of Beau Spinnaker brushing snow from the shoulders of his overcoat. 'The weather's vicious out there. Good chance we'll be snowed in later.' Charles was about to offer his words of advice on the weather when Beau noticed the Baker twins. 'You two! What on earth were you playing at last night? There could have been a very nasty accident.'

Billy pulled on Bobby's sleeve. 'We have to go now.'

Charles raised his eyebrows. 'But what about your turkey? We hadn't finished our conversation.'

Billy was already at the door with Bobby in tow. 'Forget about the turkey. We have a job to do.'

The door closed behind the boys, and Charles raised his hands in the air. 'Boys will be boys. Now, what can I do for you, Mr Spinnaker?'

Beau stood at the window, watching the twins kicking the snow as they headed towards the theatre. 'I just popped in to advise I'll be staying at least another night, so there's no need for the suits to be ready until tomorrow.' Beau nodded towards the window. 'I take it you know those boys.'

Charles edged towards the window too. 'Yes, I do. They're the Baker twins – Billy and Bobby. I'd describe them as mischievous with good hearts. They just came in to let me know they don't have a turkey for Christmas; they're very upset about it. Always hungry, those two. I keep a supply of biscuits in the storeroom for their visits.'

Beau's pale blue eyes twinkled. 'I'd like to help. Do you know where I could get a turkey from this close to Christmas around here?'

Charles rubbed his chin. 'Well, the supermarket twelve miles away was advertising fresh turkeys on the radio yesterday.'

Beau rubbed his hands together. 'Great! No need to worry about the boys. I'll solve their turkey problem.'

Charles was shocked by the man's kindness. 'That's very good of you, Mr Spinnaker. Oh, and your suits will be ready by four o'clock this afternoon, as promised. We'll be closing after that for Christmas.'

*

At five o'clock, Billy and Bobby ran through the foyer of the theatre. They burst through the revolving door straight into the path of Beau. 'Whoa! We'll have to stop meeting like this. What are you two running away from this time?'

Billy was getting fed up with this outsider who appeared intent on keeping them in line. 'Nothing.'

Bobby blushed. 'Nothing.'

The twins slowed their pace as they walked down the road away from the theatre. Beau called after them. 'I hear you need a turkey.'

Bobby turned round. His stomach sank when he remembered the turkey. Billy stopped walking and turned to stare at Beau, who was opening a taxi door. 'Well, there's been a special delivery.' Beau gestured to the children to join him. In the front seat of the taxi sat a turkey – strapped in by a seatbelt.

Bobby threw a hand to his mouth, and Billy sighed. The turkey was the least of their problems now they'd performed Lucy's backup plan. Beau bent down and looked the boys in their eyes. 'Now, the turkey's yours if you tell me what Lucy's planning to do in order to get her job back.'

Bobby held out a large clump of hair. 'It's too late. She made us cut off Prince Charming's man bun. There won't be a show tonight now, and when we get caught, we'll be in so much trouble.'

Beau squirmed. He took hold of the clump of hair and tried to keep his composure. 'Well done, boys. You've told me the plan, so the turkey's yours. Where's Prince Charming now?'

Billy decided the stranger was nice after all. 'He's asleep in his dressing room.'

'Well, don't go too far away. I'll try to salvage things. You won't get told off. Lucy's the one who's in trouble.'

The boys unbelted the turkey and lifted it from the taxi. 'Thank you, Mister; our mum will be so pleased. Happy Christmas!'

10

ANOTHER PERFORMANCE

Beau sat in the front row of the audience, tucking into a carton of popcorn. Who would have believed that Prince Charming had been wearing a wig? Or that he'd be so understanding of a schoolboy prank. It became apparent that Marcus had been a wild child in his youth. Beau sat back and watched Ellie shine on the stage; from chef to Cinderella – Ellie was amazing.

The second half of the performance was nowhere near as enjoyable – Prince Charming was in every scene. Beau was sure Ellie preferred Marcus as a blonde. She didn't take her eyes off him for a minute. Billy and Bobby took every opportunity to wave to Beau from the wings; he was a useful friend to have. They were disturbed though when they saw Lucy walk along in front of the stage and take the seat next to Beau. She had a choice of every other seat in the row – why did she choose that one?

Lucy sighed before whispering, 'I've had an awful day. Fancy a drink later?'

Beau leant to his left to move away from Lucy, who was invading his space. There was nothing he wanted less, but he couldn't find a reasonable excuse. He planned to stay another two days then head home on the morning of Christmas Eve. He hoped Lucy would have given up on trying to get her job back by then. Now, wait a minute, what was the saying? *Keep your friends close, but your enemies closer.* He was bound to bump into Lucy over the next couple of days – maybe he could use that to Ellie's advantage.

Beau smiled. 'There's nothing I'd like more.'

*

There were two tables for two in Archie's Alehouse that evening. Beau hadn't had time to eat before the show, and Lucy had lost her appetite earlier. She was getting it back now, though – Beau was a very attentive date.

'I'm sorry I was rude to you and your father the other night. I've had a lot on my mind recently.'

Beau noticed Ellie staring at him from the corner of

his eye. Was she going to have dinner with Marcus every night? Surely there was no need for that. He reached over and patted Lucy's hand. 'There's no need to apologise; you have every right to be annoyed. I can quite see how you would make a better Cinderella than Ellie. It sounds like you got caught up in an unfortunate chain of events.'

Lucy ran her fingers through her long blonde hair. 'What am I going to do, Beau? This place is dead at the best of times. The Amateur Dramatics Society has been my saviour – Eleanor always ensures I get a starring role.'

Beau frowned. 'Why would she do that?'

Lucy shrugged. 'Because there's no competition. If she doesn't keep me happy, then she wouldn't have a job. It's just unfortunate that Ellie decided to show her face as my understudy for the pantomime. She should have stayed in the kitchen.' Lucy turned to see Ellie staring at Beau, and a thought crossed her mind. She leant forward to hold Beau's hand before whispering, 'If you help me, I could be back in the role by Boxing Day, just in time to sweep the latest Prince Charming off his feet – he's Italian, you know.'

Beau pulled his hand away. 'What would I need to do?'

Lucy shielded her mouth with a menu. 'Ellie keeps

staring at you – she fancies you. Why don't you make her an offer she can't refuse? You could take her away somewhere exotic for Christmas and New Year.'

Beau sat back in his chair and glanced at Ellie. She *was* staring at him. Maybe Lucy had just concocted a perfect solution.

Ellie turned her attention from Beau to Marcus. 'What will you be doing for Christmas? Where will you go after the performance on Christmas Eve?'

Marcus lowered his eyes. 'I offered to do the worst slot out of the three of us. There won't be any Christmas for me. Luke's partying in Biarritz and Antonio's spending Christmas in Naples before flying here on Boxing Day morning. There won't be a chance for me to get to Edinburgh in time for Christmas, so I've booked to stay here at Archie's Alehouse until Boxing Day.'

Ellie reached for Marcus's hand and was pleased to note that Beau witnessed her move. 'You poor thing. I can't get home for Christmas either – but that comes as part of my job as a chef.' Ellie had an idea. 'Lord and Lady Featherlow are so kind to the staff at Christmas. I'll be back in the kitchen on Christmas Day and, when we've finished lunch duties, I'll be preparing Christmas dinner for the staff – you could join us.'

Marcus's eyes lit up. 'Are you sure? Won't the Lord

and Lady mind?'

Ellie shook her head. 'Not at all. They're just so pleased I'm cooking on Christmas Day and that Francesca can get back to Archie at the Alehouse. I've left them in the lurch for three weeks, but they haven't complained once.'

Marcus pulled Ellie towards him and planted a kiss on her cheek. 'Well, I'll be delighted to accept your offer.'

Beau's phone vibrated. He read the text message:

> *I'm at the dreaded Chronicle Christmas Party again. Just make sure you're home by five o'clock on Christmas Eve. I've invited the neighbours for our annual drinks evening. You know how important Christmas is to me, so don't be late. Mother.*

Beau gave a wry smile. He wouldn't be going home for Christmas Eve; he'd be on a plane to somewhere exotic with Ellie. That was tomorrow's job: Find a Christmas/New Year holiday Cinderella couldn't resist. He was sure Lucy would cover at the theatre on Christmas Eve too. She could do one night with Marcus before the Italian stallion arrived on Boxing Day. From now on, things were just about Beau and Ellie. He'd missed his chance once, and he was determined not to miss it again.

Marcus helped Ellie on with her coat. 'The weather's getting worse out there; let me walk you to Featherlow Manor.'

Ellie smiled brightly. 'It's only a short distance, up a lane, but Lady Featherlow insists I have transport back each night. It will be waiting outside.'

Ellie and Marcus opened the pub door to the sight of the local farmer standing next to two white horses attached to a sleigh. Ellie chuckled. 'I know! This is soooo random! The lane keeps getting blocked with the heavy snowfall, so this is the best way for me to travel.'

Marcus laughed as he tucked Ellie into the red sleigh with a fake fur blanket. Beau was now standing inside the pub's bay window. This wasn't on! Who did Marcus think he was? He brushed his sleeve up and down on the window. Condensation was blocking his view. Snow was falling in huge flakes, and Cinderella looked mesmerised by Prince Charming. The countdown to Christmas ticked away in his head: Tomorrow was the 22nd of December. That meant just two more performances at the theatre for Ellie. By Christmas Eve, she would be whisked away by someone much more appealing than Prince Charming – her old flame, Beau.

11

A SURPRISE VISITOR

How long could it take to book a holiday? It was now four o'clock in the afternoon, and Beau had spent seven hours trying to plan a late Christmas vacation. He was coming to realise it wasn't just that everywhere had been booked for months; it was the ever-worsening weather that made going away this Christmas impossible. There was nothing else for it; get through Christmas at Archie's Alehouse, then sweep Ellie off her feet as soon as the weather improved.

The sound of laughter from outside caught Beau's attention. The Baker twins were having a snowball fight with Charles, and Ellie was caught in the crossfire. 'Take it easy, boys! I'm struggling to walk along the embankment as it is. I've never known snow this deep before.'

Charles held up a hand to stop the snowball throwers. 'Let Ellie get past; then we'll continue.'

Beau grabbed his coat. What a perfect opportunity to bump into the woman of his dreams. He wished he had more suitable footwear, but his trainers would have to suffice. It was either those or his black patent lace-ups; he wound a red cashmere scarf around his neck and ran down the stairs. Charles looked up as the pub door opened. 'Mr Spinnaker! You're still here.'

Beau waved to Ellie. He hoped she could hear his words to Charles. 'Yes. I'm snowed in for Christmas, can you believe it? Luckily, Archie's Alehouse can accommodate me.'

Ellie trudged through the snow until she reached the path that Archie had cleared outside the pub. She stood before Beau in her fluorescent pink wellies. 'You need a pair of these. I don't know what I'd have done without them this week.'

Beau looked down at his trainers. 'I'm managing. I wore my trainers to get to the theatre last night and changed into my shoes when I got there. I'll do the same again tonight.'

Ellie frowned. 'You'll be there again tonight? You've already seen the show twice.'

Beau blushed. 'Well, there's nothing else to do whilst I'm stranded here.'

Ellie laughed. 'Are you sure you can't get home for Christmas?'

Charles was thinking the same thing. If Beau could get to the nearest town, he could surely afford to pay for a taxi to take him to London. The trains might not be running, but the motorways were clear. Charles was about to come up with that suggestion before he sensed Beau's awkwardness. Did the young Mr Spinnaker have a crush on Ellie Floris? It wouldn't hurt to give a good customer of Featherlow Forbes Menswear a helping hand. 'Mr Spinnaker's quite right not to risk the journey. What's so bad about spending Christmas in Featherlow Bottom? There's nothing quite like it. Especially when it snows.'

The group's attention was diverted to a man walking over the ornate footbridge spanning the river. He'd overheard their conversation. 'That's what I thought! I'm back. Hello, Cinderella.'

Ellie threw a hand to her mouth. 'Luke!' Not only had Luke returned, but he was also pulling a sledge with a large box on top.

Billy and Bobby jumped up and down in excitement. 'What's in the box?! What's in the box?!'

Luke shrugged. 'Just my clothes and a few bits and

pieces. I've had to walk the last five miles. It was a good way to keep things dry.'

Ellie held her hands in the air. 'Why aren't you in Biarritz?'

'Flight was cancelled. Is the pantomime still on in this weather?'

Ellie nodded. 'Yes. The cast members are from the village, except for you and Marcus, of course. Most of the people in the audience are local too.' Ellie glanced at Beau. 'There *is* an exception. Have you met Beau Spinnaker? He's stranded here and a regular in the front row this week.'

Luke held out his hand to shake Beau's. 'Henry Spinnaker's son, I presume. I've heard you'll be taking over from your father. Aren't you a chef? That's a big career change for you.'

Charles raised an eyebrow. So that's why the chef needed a lounge suit. Ellie shot a glance at Beau. 'You're doing what?!' Luke frowned. Why was Ellie so bothered?

Beau slipped his arm through Ellie's. 'Come with me. We need to talk.'

Luke watched as the couple disappeared into Archie's Alehouse. His heart sank. Ellie must know Beau from her time in London. Maybe they had worked together as chefs. They had a lot in common. Luke's shoulders slumped; he had nothing in common with Ellie – apart from a magical week on the stage.

Billy pulled on Luke's trouser leg. 'What's in the box?'

Luke looked up at the darkening sky. 'I'll show you tomorrow. You boys need to head off to the theatre it's getting dark.'

Charles rubbed his hands together. 'And it's far too cold to be standing around out here. There's more snow on the way.' He held out his hand to shake Luke's. 'I'm Charles. I manage the showroom for Featherlow Forbes Menswear. I understand you were Prince Charming last week.'

Luke took hold of Charles's hand. 'I'm to be Prince Charming next week too. There's no way Antonio will get here from Naples.'

Charles frowned. 'You never know. A thaw is forecast for Boxing Day. He might just make it.'

Luke shook his head. 'He definitely won't make it.' Luke pressed a finger to his lips. 'We've done a deal.'

Charles raised his eyebrows. 'What deal?'

'We're both getting engaged over Christmas. Antonio in Naples and me, well . . .'

Charles squeezed Luke's hand. 'Do I take it you have eyes for Ellie Floris?'

Luke nodded. 'We have chemistry.'

Charles nodded towards the pub. 'I think you may have some competition.'

Luke grinned. 'I gather that. May the best man win.'

12

CONFESSIONS

Ellie clasped her hands around a mug of hot chocolate whilst Beau sipped his brandy. 'I've told you, Ellie. That loser out there has got it wrong. OK, my father wants me to join the family firm – he even thinks I'm going to take over from him. That's one of the reasons I'm hiding out here.'

Ellie narrowed her eyes. 'You have no spine, Beau Spinnaker. I thought you were the one until you fired me.'

Beau sighed. 'I thought you were the one too. I thought you would understand. I had to help my father out by recruiting the son of his Finance Director. It's just unfortunate he was a chef like you. Things didn't need to end between us. You got another job straight away.'

Ellie's anger returned. 'You never wanted to talk about your father. I didn't even know who he was. How on earth have you got yourself into this position?'

Beau dropped his head. 'He threatened to cut me out of his Will.'

Ellie cringed. This wasn't the Beau she'd fallen in love with. *That* Beau had a mind of his own. He was strong, confident, driven, and at the top of his profession as a chef. She sighed. 'Well, it sounds to me your life's in a mess.'

Beau grabbed hold of Ellie's hand. 'You're right – it is! I just need to know your plans; then I'll work out what to do with mine. We could go away straight after Christmas and spend some time focusing on our future.'

Ellie pulled her hand away before laughing. 'You are no longer part of my life. My plans won't affect yours. You have such a cheek! I'm on the stage until the 2nd of January – have you forgotten about that?'

Beau held onto Ellie's shoulders and stared into her eyes. 'I'm worried about you. Lucy wants her job back. I want to take you away so that you don't get hurt. If you won't go away with me, why don't you let Lucy be Cinderella from Boxing Day? She'll stop plotting to bring you down then.'

Ellie felt a pang of guilt. Did Beau still have feelings

for her? Maybe his intentions were good. She also felt guilty about being away from her job at Featherlow Manor. If Lucy wanted her role back as Cinderella, then it made sense to let her have it. Ellie made a decision. 'You're right. I'll put Lucy out of her misery and let her return to the role from Boxing Day. That's one problem solved. The other problem is you – and it's two-fold.'

Beau blushed. 'You're right. I'm just one big problem. Can you help me?'

Ellie nodded. 'Firstly, you're invited for Christmas dinner at Featherlow Manor on Christmas Day with the staff – on the condition you help me with the cooking. I can't let you spend Christmas Day in the pub on your own. Secondly, I'll take time to help you sort out the mess you're in with your father; we need to establish the best career path for you to take. First and foremost, it has to work for *you*.'

Beau wrapped his arms around Ellie and kissed her cheek. 'I love you, Ellie Floris.'

Ellie wriggled free before giggling. 'I'm only doing this for old time's sake. I need to get to the theatre now. I'll let Eleanor break the news to Lucy that my last performance will be on Christmas Eve.'

Beau's heart was pounding. 'I'll be there in the front row for your last three shows. Any chance of lunch tomorrow?'

Ellie glanced over her shoulder. 'Don't push it.'

Beau ran up the stairs to his room above the pub. He went straight to his case and took out a pale blue leather box. He flicked it open to the sight of a large solitaire diamond ring. Admittedly, it hadn't been bought for Ellie; Beau thought he'd moved on from her – but these last few days, he realised he hadn't. That was something else Beau needed to do – break off his relationship with his father's personal assistant; now that was going to be awkward. Thank goodness Featherlow Bottom was off the beaten track. It was the perfect hideaway whilst he turned his life around.

*

Luke pulled the sledge into his room at Archie's Alehouse and went to draw the curtains. From the window, he could see Ellie's fluorescent wellies trudging through the snow. Luke smiled at the sight before a knock on his door made him jump. The handle turned, and Marcus stood in the doorway. 'So, the wanderer has returned. I thought you were in Biarritz.'

Luke grinned at his friend. 'It's a long story, but the crux of it is that Antonio's stranded in Naples, so I'll cover for him from Boxing Day. How has the pantomime been going? Any bad reviews since you took over from me?'

Marcus walked over and slapped Luke on the back. 'Only good reviews when *I* perform. I can quite see how Ellie's won your affection. Did you pop over to Naples to tie Antonio to a monument? There must be a good reason he can't make the show next week.'

Luke laughed. 'It's all about the weather. I couldn't get to Biarritz, and Antonio can't get out of Italy. Simple as that.'

Marcus glanced at his watch. 'Well, I need to head off to the theatre. Does Ellie know you'll be taking over from Antonio?'

Luke shook his head. 'Don't tell her. It's a surprise. I'll pop along to see Eleanor in the morning to go via the formal route. I'm whacked tonight.' Luke nodded at the sledge with large box. 'I pulled that thing for five miles through the snow to get here. I'll be having an early night.'

Marcus's eyes widened. 'You *have* got it bad! Don't worry; I'll keep shtum. We can catch up at breakfast. It'll be like a mini-holiday staying here together. See you in the morning, buddy!'

*

Eleanor ended the call before glancing at Ellie. 'Lucy's delighted. I have to say; I'll miss working with you,

Ellie. You haven't been any trouble at all.'

*

Ellie's mind was distracted. Did Beau say he "loved her" earlier? Surely not. She felt as if she was walking on air during the pantomime that night. Beau took every opportunity to smile at her or wave from his seat in the front row. It wasn't until the final scene – the wedding reception bun fight which Luke had created – that she remembered he was back. Why on earth had Luke travelled to Featherlow Bottom for Christmas? Why had he walked five miles through the snow, pulling a sledge? A smile lit up Ellie's face. Was Luke back because they had chemistry?

The audience rose to its feet – another standing ovation. Ellie curtseyed – she would miss this every night. Just two performances left, then she would be back to working in the kitchen. Still, working over Christmas at Featherlow Manor would be a pleasure rather than a chore. She must remember to invite Luke for Christmas dinner too.

13

WHAT'S IN THE BOX?

Luke tucked into sausages, eggs, and bacon as he listened to Marcus give an update on last night's performance. 'So, there you go – another standing ovation. You didn't need to go off-script to please the audience. Things will be different for your next stint; Cinderella won't be so accommodating of your quirky traits next time.'

Luke grinned. 'Oh, she will. We have chemistry.'

Marcus frowned. Surely not? He couldn't imagine anyone having chemistry with Lucy. He was about to interrogate Luke further when they were interrupted by the Baker twins.

Bobby leant on the table. 'What's in the box? You

said you'd tell us today.'

Luke wiped his mouth on a serviette. 'I certainly did, and I never go back on a promise. Just give me five minutes to pop upstairs. I'll be back soon.'

The twins squeezed themselves onto Luke's chair and stared longingly at a slice of toast on Marcus's plate. Marcus raised an eyebrow. 'Are you two hungry?'

The boys nodded dolefully. Marcus picked up the toast and bit into it; he watched as their sadness turned to annoyance. These were the pranksters who'd severed his man bun. It wouldn't hurt for them to feel a little pain.

Luke walked back into the room carrying a sack. The boys jumped up and stood before him. Bobby beamed. 'You look like Father Christmas.'

Luke shook his blonde curls. 'I hope not. I'm far too young to be Father Christmas.' He was pleased to note the twins were wearing their hats, scarves, and gloves this morning. He felt in his coat pocket for his own woolly hat. Luke put the sack down whilst he pulled the hat over his ears. 'Come along; we have a job to do.'

The boys glanced at one another. They'd given up doing "jobs" for people – well, at least until after Christmas. Doing "jobs" always got them in trouble. Luke threw the sack over his shoulder and headed down the embankment with the twins in tow.

Billy shoved his gloved hands into his pockets as they trudged through the snow. 'Where are we going?'

Luke glanced over his shoulder. 'To find Eleanor.'

The boys responded in unison: 'But she won't be at the theatre until this afternoon.'

Luke smiled. 'I know that. That's why we're going to see her at home to tell her my idea.'

'What's your idea?'

'I need to tell Eleanor first; then everything will fall into place.'

The trio continued their walk down the embankment towards the boat-house in the woods. Ellie had advised Luke that Eleanor lived with old sailor Sam next to the river. Luke's breath was taken away when he saw it. The house was exquisite. It had port-holes for windows and a wooden boat outside filled with mechanical elves who were busy making presents for Santa. It was dark in the woods, and an array of fairy lights twinkled in the trees. Luke knocked on the door, and Sam opened it. 'Well, well, well. Prince Charming and the Baker twins. What can I do for you?'

Luke's eyes gleamed. 'What a magical place you live in.'

Sam shuffled his feet. 'It's all Eleanor's doing. She's spruced things up a bit since she moved in. I never bothered much with Christmas before. A chicken on Christmas Day was always a treat for me. Still, Eleanor's the creative type – far beyond me to clip her wings.'

Eleanor appeared in the doorway. 'Goodness me, Sam. Aren't you going to ask our visitors in? It's freezing outside.'

Billy and Bobby burst into the boat-house. They'd been inside many times before. Usually when Eleanor was at work and Sam was at home. The twins were lucky to have Sam at the boat-house and Charles at the posh shop; it gave variety to the type of biscuits on offer.

Sam bent down and slapped his thighs. 'How about a game, you two?'

Billy and Bobby punched the air, and Sam reached under the coffee table for his box of dominoes. Luke followed Eleanor into the kitchen. Eleanor filled the kettle and peered over her shoulder. 'I heard you were back.'

Luke rubbed his hands together. 'It's fate, Eleanor. I've never met anyone like Ellie before. We have chemistry.'

Eleanor waited for the kettle to boil whilst avoiding

Luke's eyes. 'Chemistry isn't all it's made out to be.'

Luke held his hands in the air. 'It's definitely fate, Eleanor. Antonio's stranded in Italy, and I'm here now to sweep Ellie off her feet for the final week of the pantomime.'

Eleanor raised her eyes to the ceiling. 'And what will you do after that?'

Luke reached into his pocket and pulled out a small box. 'I'll ask her to marry me.'

Eleanor shrugged her shoulders. Theatre people were always over-dramatic. 'I take it there's a ring in there?'

'There certainly is. I chose it especially for Ellie at the airport when my flight to Biarritz was cancelled.'

Eleanor steeled herself. 'Did I hear correctly that you will be covering for Antonio for the final week?' Luke nodded, and Eleanor continued, 'Well, you will be Prince Charming to Lucy then. Ellie finishes her stint tomorrow night; she'll be back in the kitchen after that.'

Luke gulped before regaining his composure. He was wise enough to know that Eleanor was trying to break him down. Well, she was wrong. Not even having to suffer Lucy for a week would take the wind out of his sails. What he felt for Ellie was real, not just something for the duration of a pantomime. 'That's fine. At least I'll be here in Featherlow Bottom to ensure Ellie has the best Christmas she could wish for.'

Eleanor frowned. 'What's in your sack?'

Luke untied the rope of the canvas sack to reveal . . . ice skates. Several pairs of small ones. 'I thought we could have fun with these.'

Eleanor rubbed her forehead. 'They're all child-size.'

Luke nodded. 'That's correct. The river's frozen over, so I thought the children from the pantomime could do some charity work.'

'Charity work?!'

'Yes. It will be a great advertisement for the theatre. We'll get Beau Spinnaker to do a write-up for The National Performing Arts Chronicle. He may as well make himself useful whilst he's stranded here.'

Eleanor pulled at her hair. 'You've lost me.'

'Just imagine the headline: *The Show that Keeps on Giving*.'

Eleanor shook her head. 'I'm still confused.'

Luke frowned. 'Unfortunately, it will be a lot of work for the wardrobe team today. They need to make a selection of outfits for tomorrow's big event: Snowmen, penguins, elves, that type of thing. We can't let the children wear their pirates' costumes; they won't be warm enough.'

'Are you expecting the children to get dressed up and skate on the river?'

'That's right. Tomorrow afternoon. What better way to spend Christmas Eve?'

'How are we going to make money? The village is cut off from everywhere due to the snow. We can't expect the villagers to fork out any more; they've been keeping the pantomime afloat. I'm so grateful for their support.'

Luke's mind was working overtime. His original idea was to impress Ellie by bringing joy to the children of the village, but now it was growing out of control. 'I have a friend in London who works for a News Channel. I'll set up a Just Giving page online and video the event tomorrow afternoon. There's a good chance we'll make it onto the Evening News.'

Eleanor gasped. 'I'll call the wardrobe team straight away.'

Luke walked back into the lounge. 'Sorry, boys. No time for dominoes. You need to practice your ice skating.'

Luke held a pair of skates aloft and the twins

jumped up with glee. 'Yessss!!! We've always wanted some of those.'

Sam reached for his coat. 'I'll come with you. I used to skate on the river as a boy. I can advise from the embankment.'

Luke sighed as he closed the boat-house door behind him. A whole week on the stage with Lucy – he could have done without that. Still, it was a minor sacrifice to make before the real happy ending. Prince Charming would find Cinderella in the kitchen – not on the stage, but at Featherlow Manor.

14

EVENT PLANNING

Lucy pushed Ellie out of the way. 'You're only Cinderella for one more show. I need to wear that dress!'

Ellie clung to the pale blue ballgown. 'But I need the dress for tonight. It's been altered to fit me.'

Lucy grabbed the dress. 'I'll make do. It'll be far too big around the waist – and too short, but that will be helpful. It won't get tangled up in my ice skates.'

'Why will you be wearing ice skates? I thought it was just the children wearing ice skates.'

'I'm going to make an appearance in advance of my return to the show from Boxing Day. Luke said we may be on television tonight. He's sending in a video. No point in you showing your face. You'll be history by tomorrow.'

Billy pressed "stop" on Charles's video camera. That was a good piece of footage to have. What a stroke of luck that Charles dabbled with making home movies. Luke was thrilled – his idea was taking off. With Charles taking responsibility for producing the video, Luke could concentrate on everything else.

Charles sat with Luke in the foyer of the theatre. 'What's your theme for this video, Luke? I need to make sure I pitch it just right.'

Luke rubbed his chin. 'I want it to be an advertisement for the Woodside Theatre. It needs to be something like: *The Show that Keeps on Giving.* I want to get across that we've stayed open throughout the bad weather; that we haven't let our audiences down; that we're the centre of the community in Featherlow Bottom, even to the point of putting on a free show for the villagers on Christmas Eve.'

Charles raised an eyebrow. 'And that the theatre supports charities?'

Luke sat back in his chair. 'That's where I'm a bit stuck. This whole thing is getting out of hand. I only wanted to impress Ellie, and now there's a good chance we'll be sky-rocketed onto the local News tonight – we could even go national. What charity should we pick?'

Charles glanced over at the Baker twins, who were taking turns using his video camera. He'd taught them the basics on one of their many visits to the Featherlow Forbes Menswear showroom. 'I'm a firm believer that charity should begin at home.'

Luke rubbed his hands together. 'Excellent! Who needs charity around here?'

Charles lowered his eyes. 'That's the problem. Some people are too proud to take it.'

Luke leant forward. 'Who are we talking about?'

Charles nodded towards the boys. 'The Baker family. They don't have two pennies to rub together. Did you know they couldn't afford a turkey this year?'

'No, I didn't. That's terrible. We must buy one for them.'

'There's no need. Beau Spinnaker was the good Samaritan in that respect. I've never seen such a big turkey. I pop round regularly to drop off vegetables from my allotment. This morning, it broke my heart when Bridget Baker said there would be no presents for the boys this year. I try to help out with a few biscuits here and there and as much of my time as they need, but no one can replace their father.'

'Where's their father gone?'

'Rumour has it he had a brief dalliance with Lucy,

and Bridget threw him out. I feel for Bridget Baker, especially as she'll soon have another mouth to feed.'

'Is she pregnant?'

Charles nodded. 'She's about to drop.'

Luke's blood boiled. Of course, it had to be Lucy at the centre of a family disaster. She was always at the centre of everything. She'd even managed to get back onto the stage from Boxing Day. Luke made up his mind there and then. He wasn't going to be Prince Charming again. Marcus was off to Edinburgh on Boxing Day, and Antonio was stuck in Naples. Without a Prince Charming, there would be no Cinderella.

The men were interrupted by a huge bouquet heading towards them. Freddie Featherlow lowered the blooms which had been concealing his blushes. 'I'm sorry, but I couldn't help overhearing. I'm shocked about Lucy – but not surprised. We need to do something to help the Baker family this Christmas, and I may have a solution.'

Charles pushed out a chair for Freddie to sit down. Freddie placed the flowers on the table before articulating his thoughts, 'Don't forget about the Featherlow Bottom Benevolent Fund. My grandparents set it up years ago. We always put any surplus funds into the account after village fetes and events. We use it to replenish old equipment, replace worn-out bunting, provide presents for the children for Santa's annual visit, that sort of thing. If the funds start creeping up, then we donate to the local hospice.'

Charles stared at Luke. 'Why didn't I think of that? That's a worthy charity to support. We could do a lot of good here.'

Luke's mind was spinning. 'When's Santa visiting this year?'

Freddie laughed. 'Today, of course. It's Christmas Eve.'

Luke checked his watch. 'It's noon now. The ice skating event is at two. Could Santa appear on the bridge over the river at three o'clock? That would be a good finale to the afternoon, and it will give Charles time to edit the footage before we send it to the News Channel.'

Luke sighed; he wasn't sure why he was doing this – it could all turn out to be a big flop. His heart sank at the thought of the two little pirates without a daddy – or Christmas presents. His blood boiled at the thought of Lucy's intervention in the devastation, and his shoulders slumped at the thought of no more magical time on stage with Ellie.

Charles nodded towards the bouquet. 'Who are the flowers for?'

Freddie picked the bouquet up. 'They're for Ellie. Marcus will present them to her after her final performance tonight.'

Luke dragged himself up. 'We'd best get on with our mission. If we get a good advertisement for the theatre and community in Featherlow Bottom – and some money into the Benevolent Fund – then at least we'll have achieved something this Christmas.'

Freddie raised an eyebrow at Charles, who put a finger to his lips as Luke shuffled off. 'Prince Charming is smitten with Cinderella, but it's not all going to plan. I'm afraid not all pantomimes have happy endings.'

15

CHARITY EVENT

Billy and Bobby wore snowmen outfits. They were warm and cosy; the wardrobe team had even got the gaps for their eyes in the right place. The only problem was that Bobby was struggling to skate. Why on earth could Billy glide down the river and even do the odd spin whilst Bobby had to hold onto Luke's hand?

No one felt more uncomfortable than Luke. He was standing on the river in a pair of Freddie Featherlow's ice skates. To make matters worse, Lord and Lady Featherlow and Freddie and his wife, Amelie, were sitting at one of the wrought iron tables on the snow-cleared grass at the edge of the ornate footbridge. An oversized red chair had been placed next to them, ready for Santa. Luke shivered; why on earth was he doing this? He had nothing in common with Ellie. She was a Michelin Star Chef here in Featherlow Bottom, and he had a blossoming career in London on the stage in the West End.

Luke tried to release Bobby from his grasp before noticing a beaming Beau Spinnaker waving from the snow-covered embankment with his arm around Ellie. Charles stood next to Beau with his video camera. Just when Luke thought things couldn't get any worse, Lucy appeared in the pale blue Cinderella ballgown. She grabbed a chair and sat down to pull on a pair of ice skates.

Bobby tugged at Luke's sleeve. 'Please don't leave me. I don't want to fall over on the ice. Everyone will laugh.'

Luke smiled down at the soggy snowman. 'Don't worry. I won't leave you.'

Lucy then took "centre stage". She stood up, tried to twirl around a few times in her ice skates on a section of snow-cleared muddy grass, then signalled to Luke to help her down onto the river. Luke could see the red light on Charles's video camera and knew they were being filmed. He held out one hand for Lucy and clung onto Bobby with the other. Once Lucy was on the ice, she skated off. She glided up and down the river several times, just far enough away to ensure she remained in camera shot.

At three o'clock, Santa pulled a present-filled sleigh over the footbridge. Luke helped Bobby onto the embankment to join the other children. He was pleased the twins would have one Christmas present each this year.

Beau Spinnaker kept hold of Ellie around her shoulders. She was grateful for his warmth; it was freezing this Christmas Eve. Not only that, but her legs were also weak at the sight of Lucy taking the limelight. Had she really given up the chance of another week on the stage for that wicked witch?

All eyes turned to the emerging sight of Marcus in his Prince Charming costume; his face was drained of colour. Luke went over to him. 'Is everything all right?'

Marcus smiled. 'I've just delivered a baby.'

Lady Featherlow's mouth fell open, had she heard correctly? 'What did you say?'

'Lucy sent me to the theatre to get into costume. On my way back, I heard screams coming from a house. I've just delivered a baby on Christmas Eve!'

Annabelle glanced over at Santa; he was now seated in the red chair surrounded by excited children. Billy and Bobby were at the front of the queue for presents. Annabelle kept her voice low, 'I take it you delivered Bridget Baker's baby; it was due any day now.' A stunned Marcus nodded. 'Is she OK? Who's with her now?'

The colour was returning to Marcus's face. 'Mother and baby are fine. Two midwives arrived within minutes of the birth; I wasn't there for long.'

Lord Featherlow walked over to shake Prince Charming's hand. 'Well done, old chap! I can't say I'd be of much use in a similar situation.' Freddie locked eyes with Amelie, and they burst out laughing.

Lucy was still skating up and down the river. 'What's going on? Have I missed something?' She tried to jump to get the focus back on her, but the ice cracked. Luckily, the river wasn't deep; Lucy only fell through to her waist. Marcus offered his hand to pull her out. Charles chuckled as he captured the scene – this would make good viewing.

*

It wasn't just the residents of Featherlow Bottom who watched the News that evening. The video had, indeed, gone national. The drinks party at the Spinnaker's was rudely interrupted by several messages sent to their guests. The most worrying one was a message sent to Henry Spinnaker from his personal assistant:

> *That loser son of yours has been on the television with his arm around another woman. You now have a choice: It's him or me. There is no way I will work with that cheat!*

Henry sighed. It wasn't a difficult decision to make. He couldn't survive without his personal assistant; she'd been with him for ten years. She also knew a few things about him his wife should never find out.

*

Lucy was mortified. She was a laughing stock. Even her parents had giggled at the sight of her falling into the river. To cap it all, she'd lost two false fingernails when Marcus roughly hauled her onto the embankment. She messaged Ellie:

> *I can't do the show for the final week – you're back on.*

*

Luke decided to advise Eleanor of his decision in person. He stood on the doorstep of the boat-house and held his breath before knocking. Sam opened the door waving a glass of rum in the air. 'Come on in. We're celebrating.'

Eleanor was dancing around the lounge and, as she went to sit down, she missed the chair. Luke rushed over to soften her fall. 'Oops! Too much sherry, I'm afraid. I must say, it's been a long time since I was in the arms of a Prince Charming.'

Luke settled Eleanor onto the sofa. 'That's what I'm here to talk about.'

Eleanor patted his hand. 'Don't worry, dear, we already know. You must be thrilled that Ellie's back in the role from Boxing Day. You'll have a clear run with her until the 2nd of January.'

Sam held his hand out to shake Luke's. 'You've got a week to sweep her off her feet. Good luck, Son. Happy Christmas!'

*

At the theatre, there was a knock on Ellie's dressing room door. She opened it to the sight of Freddie Featherlow holding a large garment bag. 'Mother sent this for you. It's a ballgown of hers. She said you'd need it for the final week.'

Ellie burst into tears. She looked over at the pale blue dress with its mud stains and soggy bottom. She'd already spent the last hour trying to dry it out with a hairdryer. 'Lady Featherlow is so kind. I can never repay her.'

Freddie handed the bag over and closed the door. He couldn't resist knocking on Marcus's dressing room on the way past – Marcus was pleased to see him. 'What am I going to do with the flowers? It's not Ellie's last performance now?'

Freddie nodded. 'That's what I've come to see you about. It's *your* last performance. Keep the flowers.'

Marcus shook his head. 'I can't do that.'

Freddie smiled. 'You must. If you don't want them, then I'm sure you'll find a good home for them.'

*

It was late when Marcus made his way back to Archie's Alehouse. The cast had thrown a small party for him at the theatre. He was walking down the road carrying the flowers when he noticed a downstairs light on in the Baker house. The curtains weren't drawn, and he could see Bridget Baker sitting by the fireplace cradling her baby girl. He tapped on the window and waved. Bridget got up and unlocked the door.

Marcus smiled. 'I have some flowers for you.' Bridget blushed – a man had never brought her flowers before. 'I'm sorry it's late, but I've just finished at the theatre.'

Bridget was pleased for the company. 'Please come in. I need to thank you for what you did today. Would you like a drink?'

Marcus headed for the kitchen. 'You sit down with the baby, and I'll fix the drinks. What would you like?'

'Oh, just something soft for me. There's some lemonade in the fridge.'

Marcus opened the fridge to the sight of a large turkey. 'What time are you putting the turkey on in the morning? I guess it'll take a few hours to cook. I've never seen one so big.'

Bridget sighed. 'I'm afraid I'm a bit behind with everything to do with Christmas. I'd usually have it stuffed by now and all the vegetables peeled. We'll have to muddle through tomorrow. Billy and Bobby are good little helpers.'

Marcus poured two glasses of lemonade and walked back into the lounge. 'Well, you're in luck. I'm one big helper, and I'm free tomorrow. I'll cook dinner. I'll get to work on the vegetables now.'

Bridget gasped. 'You can't do that.'

'Why not? I was only invited to the Featherlow Manor staff Christmas dinner because Ellie felt sorry for me. I'll be of much more use here.'

Bridget blushed again. 'Well, another pair of hands would be much appreciated. Thank you so much.'

Marcus raised his glass. 'Happy Christmas, Bridget! I'll make sure it's a good one.'

16

CHRISTMAS MORNING

Beau arrived at Featherlow Manor at seven o'clock. He'd borrowed a pair of wellies from Archie for the trudge up the snow-covered lane. He was determined to be indispensable to Ellie today. What could Luke offer on Christmas Day in the kitchen? Beau thought for a second – nothing! Today Beau was going to win Ellie's heart with his Michelin Star skills. She had far more in common with him than an actor.

It crossed Beau's mind he should contact his parents to wish them a Happy Christmas, but he decided against it. He'd had several missed calls from them last night and also a number from his girlfriend. He hadn't bothered listening to the messages – today was going to be a good day, and nothing was going to spoil it. He'd put his phone in his case back at Archie's Alehouse and zipped it up – but not before taking out the box with the large solitaire diamond ring. If today went as he expected it would, he might get down on one knee.

Giles opened the manor house door before Beau could ring the bell. 'I hear you're working in the kitchen today. You need to go to the servants' entrance. Just go back down the steps and follow the building around to your right. You'll see Ellie through the kitchen window; she's been working since six.'

Beau felt well and truly put in his place. Had Giles forgotten the Spinnakers were VIP customers of Featherlow Forbes Menswear? Beau felt not the slightest bit of guilt that he hadn't made it home for Christmas with the new suits. It wasn't *his* fault the weather was so bad. He'd blame the weather for not being able to use his phone too – the signal was shocking in these remote parts at the best of times.

Beau opened the kitchen door to the sound of Christmas carols. Ellie was humming away. 'Oh, good, you're here. I love to hear carols on Christmas morning, don't you?'

Beau cringed; he detested the sound of any music in the kitchen. 'Yes. I certainly appreciate a good Christmas carol.'

Ellie put the finishing touches to a breakfast tray, and Giles appeared from the hallway to collect it. 'I'll take this straight up to Luke.'

Ellie beamed, and Beau's eyes were on stalks. 'Luke?! Did Luke stay here overnight?'

Ellie nodded. 'Lord and Lady Featherlow insisted. He was working late into the night with Freddie. The paint should be dry now. It's so exciting.'

'What paint?'

'The paint on Freddie's old wooden trainset.'

'Why were they painting a trainset?'

'I don't know if I should say. It's quite a sad story.'

'Go on, you can tell me.'

'Bridget Baker couldn't afford Christmas presents for Billy and Bobby this year, so Luke and Freddie have spruced up an old trainset, and they're going to wrap it up after breakfast.' Ellie's eyes glistened. 'They couldn't afford a turkey either.'

Beau held his shoulders back. 'I bought them a turkey. It was the largest one in the shop.'

'Oh, I heard about that. Marcus says it's in the oven already.'

'How would Marcus know?'

'He's helping the family out today. It's a bit much to expect Bridget to cook when she's just had a baby. It's a shame he won't be joining us, but we all understand he's needed elsewhere.'

Lord Featherlow entered the kitchen in his dressing gown. 'This calls for champagne! It's never too early for champagne! Where's Giles?'

Ellie stood to attention. 'Giles has just taken breakfast up to Luke. I'll get the champagne.'

The Lord glanced at Beau. 'You still here? I thought you'd be back home for Christmas. What about the suits? Freddie said you bought five.'

Beau felt humiliated. How could Winston Featherlow speak to him like he was a spare part? A redness crept up his neck and onto his cheeks when he realised he was just that – a spare part. 'My father bought four suits; I chose just the one.'

Ellie came in with the champagne. 'Beau's doing me a huge favour; he's helping me cook today. Francesca did a brilliant job with lots of prep work yesterday. It's now down to Beau and me to provide you with a Michelin Star Christmas.'

Winston turned his gaze from Ellie to Beau and back again. He chose not to share his thoughts. He was well aware of the saying: *Too many cooks spoil the broth*. Thankfully, there wouldn't be any broth today. He wondered who would take on the role of Head Chef and allowed himself a little chuckle. Nothing was going to spoil his excellent mood. He rubbed his hands together at the sight of Giles. 'How is Luke this morning?'

Giles reached for the champagne to open it. 'He looks a bit tired.'

Winston tutted. 'That's not surprising with everything he's done for this village. You could have knocked me down with a feather when I viewed the Just Giving page this morning. Make sure you set a place for him in the dining room for lunch. He'll be joining our family for the festivities.'

The champagne cork popped, and Giles enquired, 'How many glasses would you like?'

'Oh, just the one for now. I'll have a little tipple before breakfast.'

Winston drank the champagne and placed his empty glass on the kitchen table. 'Don't any of you tell Lady Featherlow. I'm supposed to be watching my cholesterol.'

*

By nine o'clock, the trainset was wrapped, and Freddie volunteered to drop it off at the Baker house. Luke scratched his head. 'I'll call Marcus and ask him to meet you outside. He'll need to find a way of getting it into the house without the boys seeing you. They'll be heartbroken by now that Santa didn't visit last night. Marcus will smooth things over.'

Lady Featherlow jumped up. 'Wait! You can't go yet.' She dashed out of the room and returned five minutes later with a porcelain doll. 'You need a present for the little girl.'

Winston raised his eyebrows. 'But that's *your* dolly, Annabelle. You can't give that away.'

Annabelle stood firm. 'Oh, yes I can, Winston. There's nothing I want to do more.'

Freddie noticed the tears in his mother's eyes. The porcelain doll had sat on her dressing room table for as long as he could remember. He could see where she was coming from, though; the baby needed a present, and all the shops were shut today. Freddie had no old toys suitable for a girl. He decided not to prolong his mother's agony. 'We'd best wrap it up then. I'll head off as soon as it's done.'

*

Christmas that morning in the Baker house was magical. The twins decided Marcus was a much better daddy than their original one. For one thing, he promised them that Santa was still on his way. He said they had to wait a bit longer for their present as their names had to be moved from the naughty list to the good list. It was just unfortunate an elf had told Santa about them cutting off Prince Charming's man bun. After much deliberation, Santa had decided to forgive them.

Sure enough, when the doorbell rang at ten o'clock, there were two presents on the doorstep. Marcus said Santa couldn't get them down the chimney because the fire was lit. Billy and Bobby ran to the window and looked to the sky for a whole five minutes to see Santa on his sleigh. Marcus stepped forward to hold the boys around their shoulders before advising them Santa would be well on his way back to Lapland by now; it was unfortunate they couldn't see him due to too much cloud cover.

The twins turned from the window before falling to their knees to rip the wrapping paper off their joint present. Bobby squealed excitedly. 'It's a trainset! A trainset with lots of track and lots of trains.'

Billy picked up a bridge. 'It's got a bridge, and a tunnel, and a station.'

Bridget stared at Marcus before whispering, 'Who bought it?'

Marcus shrugged. 'Santa.' He handed the other present to Bridget. 'This is for the little lady. You will need to unwrap it for her.'

Bridget carefully removed the wrapping paper and opened the box to reveal a silver rattle. Her eyes filled with tears. 'Everyone has been so kind.'

*

Freddie strode back up the lane; he was looking forward to Christmas dinner. How kind of Giles to find the rattle; he said it had been in one of the kitchen drawers for years. When Freddie got back to the manor, he would put the porcelain doll back on his mother's dressing room table. He couldn't wait to see the relief on her face when she realised it had returned.

17

CHRISTMAS DINNER

The Featherlows always ate dinner at three o'clock on Christmas Day. That gave time for the staff to eat theirs at five o'clock before they prepared an evening buffet for the family. A buffet sufficed after a large turkey meal with all the trimmings. Annabelle walked into the dining room and headed straight over to Freddie. 'My doll's back. Why didn't you give it to the baby?'

Freddie grinned. 'We all know how much that doll means to you. Giles came up with an alternative present.'

'What?'

'A silver rattle. Giles said it had been in the kitchen drawer for years.'

Annabelle frowned. 'I wonder whose it was?'

Freddie pulled a chair out for his mother. 'Does it matter? It's of far more use now than it was hidden away in the kitchen.'

*

The turkey lay on a large silver platter, surrounded by sprigs of holly. Beau grimaced. 'Why on earth have you put holly around the turkey?'

Ellie smiled. 'It's a tradition of the family. Apparently, Lord Winston put holly around the turkey when he was a toddler. They've done it ever since.'

Beau placed the platter on a trolley. 'I'll wheel it in. I can explain the different types of stuffing parcels. A good idea of mine, don't you think, to tie them up with sprigs of rosemary?'

Ellie shrugged her shoulders. 'Each to their own. I'd have presented the stuffing differently.'

Giles stepped forward to take the trolley, and Beau shooed him away. 'There's no need for that. It's good for the chef to take the turkey in.' Beau winked at Giles. 'It's a way of getting a pat on the back.'

*

Winston raised an eyebrow as Beau gave an account of the ingredients in the stuffing parcels. So, Beau

Spinnaker had taken on the role of Head Chef. Winston wasn't a fan of people taking the limelight away from those who deserved it more. 'Where's my carving knife? Giles always brings it in with the turkey?'

Giles entered the room with the knife, and Winston stood up. 'Good man, good man. Bring that turkey over here so that I can reach. Thank you for helping out today, Beau. You can return to the kitchen now.'

It wasn't long before Winston was waving a pricked finger in the air. 'Drat! I do that every year. Not a great idea of mine to put holly around the turkey in the first place. Still, I was only a tiny terror at the time.'

Freddie's wife, Amelie, burst out laughing. 'You – a tiny terror?! I can never imagine that.'

Winston carried on carving. 'Oh, I was always getting into trouble. None more so than when I lost my silver rattle; it was a family heirloom and worth a fortune. I was sure I put it on the platter whilst I demolished my mother's table arrangement. I pulled the holly out because I liked the look of it, all shiny with red berries. I thought it would go well with the turkey.'

Amelie giggled. 'You weren't planning to eat the holly, were you?!'

Winston shook his head. 'Of course not. I just

thought the turkey looked dull; a bit of greenery around it set it off a treat.'

Freddie raised his eyebrows at his mother, who had turned a bright shade of pink. 'Oh, my goodness, it's hot in here. Open a window, please, Giles.'

Winston was still reminiscing, and Annabelle stared at the butler before mouthing the words: 'Say nothing – just open the window.'

Luke twisted in his seat. He'd much rather be having dinner with Ellie in the kitchen; maybe he could have two dinners. There was a thought; he wouldn't eat too much at this one, then he'd have some room to join the staff at five o'clock.

*

With their first chance to take a break, Ellie and Beau wrapped up warm and ventured outside. There was nowhere to speak in private in the kitchen, and Ellie had promised to help Beau sort his life out.

'So, you're telling me your father will cut you out of his Will if you don't join the family business?' Beau nodded. 'But you have two brothers and a sister, can't they help out?'

'That's just the problem. Father's already coerced them into working for him. I'm the one with an eye for success. He needs me. He knows I'll make a good job of anything I turn my hand to. I just can't help it that I prefer restaurants to theatres.'

Ellie threw a hand to her mouth, and Beau stared at her. 'What?'

'I've had a brilliant idea.'

'What?'

'Don't restaurants and theatres go together? I mean, most people have dinner before or after a show, don't they?'

'Well, yes.'

'There you are then. You could add another string to your father's bow. When you join the business, you can spice things up a bit.'

'I don't know what you mean.'

'How about changing the name of The National Performing Arts Chronicle to: The National Guide to Performing Arts & Cuisine – or something like that?'

Beau scratched his head, and Ellie continued, 'You could even open your own restaurants near to theatres. If you don't want to be stuck in an office, just get a good team working for you whilst you do the job you enjoy. That way, your father's business will expand, and you won't be cut out of his Will.'

Beau's eyes filled with tears, and he threw his arms around Ellie. 'You're good for me, Ellie. You've always had my best interests at heart. That's why I need you.' Beau's tears soon turned to laughter, and he punched the air. Luke watched the scene unfold through the dining room window. What on earth was Beau Spinnaker playing at?

Beau felt there was no time like the present. He bent down on one knee in the snow and pulled the ring box out of his pocket. 'Marry me, Ellie.'

As Ellie took a step backwards, her welly caught on a snow-covered kerb, and she fell flat on her back. Luke jumped out of his seat. 'Please excuse me.' He dashed out of the dining room and was at Ellie's side before Beau could brush the snow from his soggy knee. 'Leave this to me. We need to check she's not badly injured.'

Ellie laughed as she waved her arms and legs about. 'There's nothing wrong with me. Look!'

Luke knelt in the snow beside her. 'Are you telling me you just wanted to make a snow angel?'

Ellie smiled. 'That's about it. Would you help me up, please? I'm a bit limited with what I can do in these wellies.'

Luke helped Ellie to her feet before swinging an arm under her legs and carrying her back to the kitchen. He whispered in her ear, 'Don't marry him.' Ellie could see Beau trailing behind with the ring box. He pushed it back into his pocket.

'Oh, I think that was just an impulse thing. Beau's strong on impulse. He'll have changed his mind before we tuck into the turkey.'

Luke kissed her cheek. 'I sincerely hope so! By the way, is there enough turkey for me? I'm not leaving you alone with that loser for another minute.'

Lord and Lady Featherlow were waiting at the kitchen door. Annabelle wrung her hands together. 'Are you all right, my dear? You gave us all a terrible fright.'

Luke placed Ellie on the chair Giles had brought to the door. Beau stood next to her, and Ellie didn't know whether to laugh or cry. She was soaking wet and needed to get changed. She was also trembling from the shock of it all. Had Beau just proposed? Did he mean it?

Winston glanced at Beau. 'I suggest you take over as Head Chef for the staff meal. Ellie did an excellent job with the family dinner. She should put her feet up for the rest of the day. Luke will look after her, won't you, Luke?'

Luke squeezed Ellie's shoulder. 'I certainly will. You don't need to worry about that.'

Winston then remembered a message he'd taken for Beau earlier in the day. 'Your father telephoned this morning. He's been struggling to get hold of you; there must be a problem with your phone. Anyway, he's asked that you give him a call. He said your girlfriend wanted a word with you too. You can use the telephone in my study if you need somewhere private.'

*

In the absence of Beau Spinnaker, Ellie carried on with the preparations for the staff meal. Luke did what he could to ease her workload. He was secretly thrilled that Ellie's ex-boyfriend had done a runner. What a spineless loser? Proposing to Ellie when he already had a girlfriend was beyond belief. Thankfully, Ellie wasn't surprised by Beau Spinnaker's under-hand antics.

At five o'clock, the staff were seated around the kitchen table, and Luke stood up to propose a toast: 'I'm sure you'll all join with me in thanking Cinderella for cooking this magnificent Christmas dinner. Tomorrow night she'll be back at the theatre preparing to go to a ball. And, for that, there's no one more grateful than me. Without Ellie's loyalty and commitment, there would have been no pantomime this year.'

Several staff members sighed and wished they'd had the chance to be on stage with Prince Charming. When Luke was standing up with them all sitting down, he looked about ten feet tall. His blonde curls swung when he moved and shone from the low hanging ceiling lights. Ellie Floris was so lucky!

18

THE RATTLE SAGA

Lady Featherlow took the opportunity of the break between dinner and evening buffet to sit in her husband's study and write a letter. Freddie saw the light on and wandered into the room to see what his mother was doing. At the sight of her son, Annabelle held her head in her hands. 'Oh, Freddie. We are in so much trouble; I remember the story of the missing rattle now. It's solid silver and was a present to a previous Lord Featherlow from the King. It's engraved with a Royal Coat of Arms.' Annabelle tutted. 'Trust your father to lose it.'

Freddie nodded towards the letter his mother was writing. 'What are you doing now?'

'I'm writing to Bridget Baker, and I need you to take her this letter without telling your father anything about it. What's done is done, and what's in the past should stay there.'

'What do you mean?'

'Don't you see? If word gets out that the Baker family has got hold of the rattle, people will come to the wrong conclusions. We can't ask for it back; that would look silly on our part, so we need to put in writing that we gave the rattle to the baby.'

Freddie felt uncomfortable about all of this, but his mother was adamant. He had an hour to spare before the evening buffet, so he took the letter and set off down the lane into the village. It wouldn't be too late to call on the Baker family; the twins would still be up. Besides, it would be good to see how Marcus was coping.

Giles was waiting for Lady Featherlow outside the study. 'I need to speak to you about the rattle.'

Annabelle held a finger to her lips. 'There's nothing for you to worry about, Giles. I've sorted everything. Now, let's change the subject. Have you decanted Lord Featherlow's favourite port for tonight? Heaven forbid if he doesn't have a glass or two before bed on Christmas Day.'

*

Marcus heard a light tapping on the front door; he

opened it to the sight of Freddie. 'I didn't like to ring the bell in case the baby was asleep.'

Marcus glanced over his shoulder at Bridget. 'It's Freddie Featherlow.'

Bridget fluffed up the cushions on the sofa. 'Oh, do ask him in.'

Freddie walked into the small front room with roaring fire and noticed the large bouquet on the coffee table. So, Marcus had chosen to give Ellie's flowers to Bridget. He looked at Marcus out of the corner of his eye. He was bending down, trying to soothe the crying baby in a crib. Freddie felt like a spare part. He was about to pull the letter out of his coat pocket when Bridget handed him the silver rattle. 'If you give this a little shake next to the crib, it'll stop her crying. I don't know what we'd have done without it today.'

Freddie did as requested and was amazed at the lightness of the rattle. He expected solid silver to weigh much more. As he was shaking it he saw a name engraved on the side. With the baby settled, Bridget took the rattle from Freddie and nodded towards the back room. 'The boys are in there playing with a trainset. Did it belong to you?'

Freddie held his hands in the air. 'Guilty! I'm afraid it needed a paint job. Luke kindly helped me last night.'

Marcus chuckled. 'Well, you two are certainly a pair

of Santa's little helpers.'

Bridged blushed. 'You've all been so kind up at the manor. Please thank everyone for me.'

Freddie gestured towards the back room. 'May I?'

Bridget nodded, and Freddie gently opened the door. Billy and Bobby were engrossed with the train set. Freddie wiped a tear from his eye. There was no better feeling than giving to others. He turned to leave. 'Well, now that we know you're all doing so well, I'll head off home. Happy Christmas, everyone!'

Bridget stared at Marcus. 'That was strange.'

Marcus rubbed his chin. 'I expect he just wanted a reason to pop into Archie's Alehouse for a quick one. Checking up on us was as good a reason as any to escape from the manor house.'

It gave Bridget a warm feeling to hear Marcus say "us". 'Why don't you pop to the pub for a quick one? Nothing's stopping you.'

It was Marcus's turn to blush. 'Only the fact that I'd rather stay here.'

Bridget lowered her eyes. 'There's a bottle of brandy at the back of the wardrobe; I'll fetch that down for later. I wouldn't want you to think we were in short supply of anything. I always provide for my family.'

*

Freddie strode up the steps to the manor, and Giles opened the door. 'Giles! Why didn't you tell us about the rattle? Mother's in bits.'

Giles held his shoulders back. 'I've been trying to tell Lady Featherlow, but she won't listen to me.' Freddie took the letter out of his pocket and ripped it up. He decided to dispose of it in the bin in the kitchen before going to see his mother.

The trolleys in the kitchen were loaded with silver platters containing the buffet food. Ellie smiled at Freddie. 'You're back! Lady Featherlow said you'd popped out, and we should hold the buffet until you returned. I'll send it up to the dining room straight away.'

Luke was sitting at the kitchen table surrounded by boxes of old Christmas decorations. He glanced up at Freddie. 'Can you believe they've not decorated the kitchen or that magnificent Christmas tree outside?'

Ellie felt a pang of guilt. 'I usually put a few decorations up in the kitchen, but this year has been so busy with the pantomime and everything.'

Luke grinned. 'Well, I've raided the pantry. Even with my height, I needed step ladders to reach the top shelf for these boxes. Some of the decorations are ancient. There are a few with your name tags on them;

you must have made them at school.'

Freddie sat down opposite Luke. 'Let me see. Oh, yes, I remember sewing that Christmas stocking. Can you sew, Luke?'

Luke shook his head. 'Not something I've ever had the pleasure of learning. It would be useful though if I split a seam in one of my costumes.' Luke frowned; what about the costumes from tomorrow? Had they been altered to fit Marcus? Luke chose not to worry; he guessed they were about the same size.

*

Freddie decided to keep hold of the stocking. He could have a laugh with everyone about it during the buffet. He walked into the dining room, holding it aloft. Annabelle threw a hand to her chest. 'Your lovely stocking! I remember when you came home from school with it that Christmas. We were so proud of you, weren't we, Winston?'

Winston placed an arm around his wife's shoulders. 'We certainly were. We've had some good times at Christmas, haven't we, my darling? This Christmas is no exception.' Annabelle tried to ignore her pricking conscience as she nodded.

*

Luke opened yet another old box. This one contained

a plastic table decoration with faded silk flowers. Luke was about to close the box when he spotted a shiny object. He delved deep into the box and pulled out a silver rattle. Luke held up a sprig of plastic holly with red berries and burst out laughing.

Ellie smiled at him. 'What are you laughing at?'

'Lord Featherlow was reminiscing at lunchtime about the time when he was a toddler. He said he pulled the holly out of his mother's table arrangement one Christmas and put it around the turkey to liven it up a bit – he lost his rattle at the same time.' Giles walked over to stand next to Luke.

Luke shook the rattle in the air. 'I thought it was a bit dangerous allowing a toddler to play with holly. Now I know why Lord Winston's mother let him demolish her table arrangement – it was plastic!'

Giles held his hand out. 'I'll give the rattle to Lady Featherlow.'

Luke held onto it. 'Why don't we have a bit of fun with it first?'

Giles stepped back, and Luke strode around the kitchen looking for a container. 'Is there a box we could put it in, so we can give it to Lord Featherlow as a gift? We could leave it by the fireplace and say Santa brought it.'

Ellie giggled. 'We're a day late for that.'

Luke scratched his head. 'Has anyone got a better idea?'

Giles put his hand up. 'I'll polish it to a shine and place it inside Lord Featherlow's cigar box. He'll retire to the drawing room later for a glass of port.'

Luke slapped Giles on the back. 'Great idea! We'll leave it to you, Giles. I want to get that tree outside decorated before the day's over. Are you sure the lights you gave me will be safe?'

Giles nodded. 'They're one of the new sets we bought two years ago. I always keep some spare.'

*

Freddie pulled his mother to one side. 'The rattle belonged to Giles. It's silver-plated and has his name engraved on the side. I vaguely remember he let me play with it in the kitchen when I was a toddler. He's been trying to tell you – but you keep shutting him down.' Annabelle let out a sigh of relief before remembering the letter. She was about to ask Freddie about it when he bent down to whisper in her ear, 'I've destroyed the letter.'

Winston led his family into the drawing room. 'Who's for port?'

Giles glanced at Lady Featherlow as he picked up

the cigar box. He held it in front of Lord Winston, who was shocked. 'Cigars before port? Well, I'm open to a change or two in tradition.' Winston opened the box. 'Well, I never! Where did you find this?'

Giles kept his composure. 'Luke found it in an old Christmas decorations box at the top of the pantry.'

Winston took hold of the rattle and shook it in the air. 'That boy is nothing short of a miracle worker. Since he's been in the village, our finances have gone through the roof. I'll have the rattle valued after Christmas. Send him up, Giles. He should join us for port and cigars.'

Giles felt Lady Featherlow's stare. He turned his gaze towards her whilst she mouthed the words: 'Sorry, Giles.'

19

A TREE TO DECORATE

Luke shook his head. 'Sorry, Giles. I don't have time to drink port or smoke cigars; I've got a tree to decorate.'

Giles raised his eyebrows. 'But Lord Featherlow has requested your attendance.'

'That's OK. Just let Lord Featherlow know I'm otherwise indisposed.'

*

Winston choked on his drink. 'Otherwise indisposed?! What can be more important than a glass of port on Christmas Day?'

Giles looked to the ground. 'Decorating a tree.'

Amelie burst out laughing. 'What tree?'

'The tree outside the kitchen.'

Winston placed his glass on the sideboard. 'This I must see.'

*

Ellie was holding the ladders for Luke when the Featherlow family appeared. Freddie dashed over. 'Here, let me help.'

Amelie slipped her arm through Annabelle's. 'Do you think Luke's trying to impress Ellie?'

Annabelle's eyes twinkled. 'Yes. I do.'

Winston rubbed at his arms. 'It's mighty chilly out here. I'll wait in the kitchen.' Annabelle decided to join him, and Amelie went inside to fetch Freddie's coat. Winston's attention was drawn to the vast amount of old boxes Luke had rummaged through to salvage decorations for the tree. He sat down at the kitchen table and had a look through the remnants of Christmas past.

'Annabelle! Look at this! I made this star out of tinsel when I was at school. Why isn't Luke putting it at the top of the tree?'

Annabelle raised her eyes to the ceiling. 'It looks a

bit fragile, Winston. Why don't we put it on one of the trees inside the manor?'

Winston was engrossed in the boxes; he handed the star to his wife. 'You take care of it whilst I see what other treasures I can find.'

Freddie was pleased when Amelie returned with his coat. 'Go inside with Ellie; Luke and I can finish this.' The girls didn't need prompting twice before retreating to the welcome warmth of the kitchen.

Freddie's breath was visible as he called up the ladder to Luke. 'Why are you doing this?'

Luke glanced down at him. 'Because I want Ellie to have a Christmas to remember.'

Winston's attention was drawn to a sheet of old newspaper. 'Well, I never. I didn't know that.' Annabelle peered over his shoulder. The newspaper was dated over forty years ago, and the headline read: *Love at First Sight*.

Annabelle gasped. 'That's Charles and Olivia on their wedding day. What a beautiful photograph.'

Amelie jumped up. 'Let me see!' She read parts of the article aloud:

> *Charles proposed to Olivia after just three days … They were married six weeks after*

their first date ... Charles said: 'When you find "the one", why wait?'

Annabelle sighed. 'How romantic!' She slapped Winston's arm. 'It took you two years to propose.'

Winston shrugged his shoulders. 'I had to get my mother's approval first. It took her a while to warm to you.'

The girls glanced at one another and burst out laughing. Ellie opened the fridge. 'I almost forgot; Beau made some chocolate liqueurs earlier. Would anyone like one?'

Freddie strode into the kitchen, followed by Luke. 'Yes, please! Hand them around.'

Luke rejected the offer when the plate reached him. Trust Beau Spinnaker to pop up just when he was about to "make a memory" with Ellie. Annabelle sensed his awkwardness. 'Well, I think we should head back to the drawing room and leave these two young people alone. They'll need a rest before they're back on stage tomorrow night.'

With the kitchen to themselves, Luke turned out the lights. He held Ellie's hand and took her to the window before pressing the button on a remote control. The lights on the tree outside exploded into a riot of twinkling colour.

Ellie threw a hand to her mouth. 'That's so lovely! What's on the top of the tree?'

Luke smiled. 'Cinderella and Prince Charming. The wardrobe team made them for me.'

Ellie laughed. 'How thoughtful.'

Luke reached for his phone and pressed "Play". The kitchen filled with music from the ballroom scene of the pantomime. Luke held out his hand. 'May I have this dance?' Ellie nodded, and the pair twirled around the kitchen table until the music stopped. Luke held a chair for Ellie to sit down and reached under the table to produce a glass slipper. He knelt on one knee and slid it onto Ellie's foot.

Ellie's heart was pounding. She felt flustered; Luke was the most exciting man she'd ever met. She didn't know what to say, except: 'It fits!'

Luke reached under the table again, this time for a small box. He gazed up at Ellie with his turquoise eyes shining. 'Will you marry me, Ellie Floris?'

Ellie caught her breath at the sight of a princess cut diamond ring. 'Are you serious?'

Luke held her gaze. 'I've never been more serious about anything in my life.'

'But we've only known each other for two weeks.'

Luke blushed. 'I have a confession to make. My flight to Biarritz wasn't cancelled. I made it to the jewellery shop at the airport and knew I had to get back to you as quickly as possible. I had to put a ring on your finger. When you find "the one", why wait?'

Ellie held out her left hand. 'Well, let's hope it fits.'

Luke slid the ring onto Ellie's finger before smiling. 'There was no doubt in my mind it would fit.'

Ellie knelt on the floor in front of her Prince Charming before throwing her arms around him. It was a risk to take – but it felt so right. Nothing was going to spoil her last magical week on the stage. Everything would fall into place after that – she was sure of it. With Luke by her side, she could do anything.

20

BOXING DAY

Luke knocked on Marcus's bedroom door. 'Wakey-wakey. It's eight o'clock, and you have a train to catch.'

Marcus climbed out of bed and opened the door. 'I was hoping for a lie-in today.'

'But you're off to Edinburgh. The trains are running again, and you'll be late.'

Marcus stretched his arms. 'I've changed my plans. I'm staying another week.'

Luke frowned. 'Well, you can't be Prince Charming. Cinderella's mine. We got engaged last night.'

Marcus shrieked. 'What?! You crafty old devil. I'll

throw on some clothes and meet you down in the bar for breakfast. See you in ten.'

Luke was sipping his coffee when Marcus surfaced. 'You're not joking, are you? I can't believe Ellie would be so reckless.'

Luke winked. 'Don't call my fiancée "reckless". She knows when she's onto a good thing. Now tell me why your plans have changed.'

Marcus fiddled with his serviette. 'I'm needed here.'

'What in the pub?'

'No! At the Baker house. Bridget has her hands full, and it's the least I can do to stay around for a bit longer. I was only going to Edinburgh for a Christmas break – I may as well spend my holiday here.'

Luke cut into his sausage. 'When do you need to be back in London?'

Marcus shrugged. 'Not for the imminent future. I didn't get the role I auditioned for before Christmas.'

Luke's spine tingled. 'Lucky you. I've been offered the role of my dreams. Rehearsals start in February.'

Marcus raised his eyebrows. 'In the West End?'

Luke nodded. 'I'll need to tell them the bad news. There's no way I'm leaving Ellie. I'll have to find a job down here.'

Archie placed two toast racks on the table. 'There's a job going here if anyone wants it. Ivan's left me in the lurch. I need someone to start straight away.'

Marcus and Luke stared at one another before Marcus held out his hand to shake Archie's. 'I'll take it. I'm available immediately.' He nodded towards Luke. 'Prince Charming over there is on the stage for another week.'

Archie frowned. 'Have you done bar work before?'

Marcus smiled. 'I've done more bar work than acting. Luke's the lucky one who gets all the roles.'

Luke grinned. 'Less of the "lucky" and more of the "talented". Fair play, mate. I hope things work out well for you.'

Marcus winked at Archie. 'Any chance of a reduced rate on my room until I'm able to sort out something more permanent?'

Archie raised an eyebrow. 'I'll see what I can do.'

*

After catching the early train to London, Beau sat opposite his father. 'I've had a brilliant idea. When I join the family firm, I'll make some changes to cater for my talents. We should bring theatres and restaurants together and expand The Chronicle's offering. Theatres and restaurants go hand-in-hand.'

Henry Spinnaker twiddled his fingers. 'I've changed my mind. You won't be joining the business. We no longer have a vacancy.'

'Are you saying you don't want me to work with you?'

Henry nodded.

'Does that mean I won't be cut out of your Will?'

Henry shook his head. 'It's not my decision; it's your mother's. You didn't make enough effort to come home for Christmas.'

Beau held his hands in the air. 'But it's only Boxing Day – I'm back now.'

Henry stood up and walked out of the room. Theatres and restaurants? What a good idea. He'd get onto it straight away.

*

Ellie sat at the kitchen table in a flood of tears. Annabelle gave her a handkerchief. 'There, there, this is supposed to be a happy time for you.'

Ellie wiped her eyes. 'I can't see how it will work. Luke's destined for a career in the West End, and he's willing to give it up for me. He's happiest when he's on the stage.'

Annabelle produced another handkerchief. 'That's not true, Ellie. He's happiest when he's with you.'

Although it pained Annabelle to say it, she knew she must. 'Have you thought about going to London with him?'

Ellie nodded. 'I've thought of everything. But I'm at my happiest here. I'm my own boss in this kitchen, and your family is just the best to work for. I couldn't take the pressure of going back to working for someone else. The London restaurant scene is cut-throat unless you're famous.'

Annabelle patted Ellie's hand. 'Now come on, wipe those tears away. There's a solution to everything. Love always finds a way.' A seed was growing in Annabelle's mind, and she went in search of her husband.

'Winston! We should go to the pantomime tonight. The Royal Box is always available to us. Why don't we eat out as well? We can give Francesca the night off.'

Winston removed his glasses. 'Where will we eat?'

'Archie's Alehouse, of course. Let's aim to get there for five o'clock.'

21

DINNER AND PANTO

Winston read the menu for a third time. 'There's not much of a selection on here, is there?'

Annabelle beamed. 'Archie does his best. Featherlow Bottom isn't exactly swarming with eateries.'

'What are *you* having? Can you choose for me too?'

When Marcus wandered over to take their order, Annabelle gasped. 'Marcus! What are you doing here?'

Marcus smiled. 'Let's just say I've fallen in love with Featherlow Bottom, and I've decided to stay. Do you know what you'd like to order?'

Annabelle read from the menu. 'I'll have the spaghetti bolognese, and my husband will have the pepperoni pizza. We'll also take two sides of garlic bread.'

Marcus retrieved the menus. 'What would you like to drink?'

Winston waved a hand in the air. 'That's my choice! We'll have a bottle of your finest claret. Thank you, Marcus.'

Winston glared at his wife. 'Why did you order me pizza?! I've never had one before. Ghastly things!'

Annabelle chose to ignore her husband. 'I must admit I'm quite enjoying this. We should do it more often.'

Winston shuffled in his seat. 'Why would we want to eat here when we have a Michelin Star Chef back at the manor? I've only come out with you tonight as Ellie's on the stage this week. The sooner she gets back to the kitchen, the better.'

Half a bottle of wine later, Annabelle made her move. 'Have you ever thought of taking on another business?'

'What business would I want to take on? I'm retired now. Freddie's holding the fort at Featherlow Forbes Menswear. I've given up a hands-on role.'

'You wouldn't need to do a hands-on role at Featherlow Floris Fine Dining; Ellie would be the boss.

You would just reap the rewards. Think of the profits from a top London restaurant – a famous restaurant at that. The Featherlow name is a worldwide brand. We could fill the restaurant with our loyal customers alone. I'm sure they all go to the theatre in the West End.'

Winston wiped his mouth. 'That pizza was jolly good.' He downed his glass of claret and poured another one before demolishing his garlic bread. Annabelle took that as a good sign – Winston was mulling her idea over. He sat back in his chair. 'But who would cook at the manor?'

'We'll easily find a top chef. Look how quickly we found Ellie. The bonus with her managing our restaurant in London will be that we can eat there whenever we like.'

Winston sipped his wine. 'It's a pity the restaurant won't be nearer to here.'

Annabelle patted her husband's hand. 'I was coming onto that. There doesn't have to be just one restaurant. If it's successful, there could be a chain. Ellie would train the staff, but the West End will be her base. Just think of the admiration it would bring. You'll not only have a global menswear business, but you'll also have a chain of restaurants too. All you need to do is fund the start-up of the first one, and everything will be plain sailing after that.'

'Don't forget my yacht. People admire me for that.'

'Of course, they do, Winston. No one will forget your yacht.'

*

At the theatre, Annabelle was surprised her husband was so cheerful. He laughed throughout the pantomime. Tears streamed down his face at some parts. 'Luke is such a good actor. I can't remember enjoying a show as much as this. Tell me again why our first restaurant needs to be in the West End?'

Annabelle came clean. 'Because Luke and Ellie are engaged, and she needs to move to London to be near him. He's a rising star.' Annabelle fanned herself with her programme. 'It'll be a win-win situation for all of us if you're prepared to make a little investment in the name of love.'

Winston raised his eyebrows. 'When did they get engaged?'

'Yesterday.'

'My investment can be an engagement present then.' Annabelle couldn't believe her ears, and Winston continued, 'Those Prince Charmings have certainly spiced things up in the village. What about Marcus? He said he'd "fallen in love with Featherlow Bottom" – he's fallen in love with Bridget Baker more like. I've been getting updates from Giles.'

Annabelle giggled. She'd telephone Archie tomorrow and arrange for a crate of his finest claret to be brought up to the manor. Her husband had never been so amenable.

*

Ellie was in shock. She sat in her dressing room wearing Lady Featherlow's ballgown, with Luke standing behind her, as they both took in the news. Lord Featherlow reiterated "his" idea once again: 'So, you see, I've been looking to invest in a new business, and what better one to throw my money at than Featherlow Floris Fine Dining in the West End. That will be the flagship restaurant. The aim will be to expand in due course – a smaller version here in Featherlow Bottom will be a priority. It's good to have ambition – people admire that.'

Annabelle stared at Ellie – she hadn't said a word. 'This will all be very shocking for you, Ellie – and Luke. Why don't you think about it and let us know your opinions in the next day or so.'

Luke squeezed Ellie's shoulder, and she turned to look into his glittering eyes. His smile told her all she needed to know. 'There's no need to think about it. I'd be delighted to accept your offer. You are both so kind.'

Winston turned to leave the dressing room. 'Does Archie's Alehouse offer post-theatre dining?'

Luke smiled. 'It certainly does. We're off there now to celebrate – would you like to join us?'

Winston rubbed his hands together. 'I wouldn't mind another pizza. Annabelle and I will head off; we'll meet you there.'

The dressing room door closed, and Ellie burst into tears. 'Did that just happen? I'm not dreaming, am I?'

Luke held her in his arms. 'You're not dreaming. Lord Featherlow is your Fairy Godfather.'

Ellie blew her nose. 'We'd best get changed then – I wouldn't want to keep him waiting.'

22

NEW YEAR'S EVE

Marcus had just finished his lunchtime shift at the pub when Archie walked out of the kitchen carrying a box full of food. 'Do you think the Baker boys could polish this lot off? We need to make more of an effort to limit any waste in the kitchen.'

Marcus thought of Bridget's limited supplies, and his eyes twinkled. 'Well, if you're sure. Those boys would eat anyone out of house and home.'

Archie nodded and lowered his eyes as he handed the box over. 'They'll be doing me a favour. I'll bear them in mind before throwing good food away again.'

*

Marcus headed down the embankment carrying the

box. He knocked on the door to Bridget's house, and Bobby opened it. 'What have you got there?'

'Oh, just some leftover food from the pub.'

Bridget sat by the fire with her baby. 'My goodness, that's very kind of Archie. Is he sure about this?'

Marcus nodded. 'Definitely. We're doing him a favour. You could say it's a "perk of the job" with me working there.'

Bobby stuck his hand into the box, closely followed by Billy. They both pulled out packets of biscuits. Looking down into the box, the boys could see boxes of cakes and sweets hidden beneath the fresh fruit and vegetables.

Billy looked at Bobby. 'Are you thinking what I'm thinking?'

Bobby grinned before turning to his mother. 'Can we have these biscuits, please? We want to give them away as presents.'

Bridget smiled. 'I don't see a problem with that. We should share our good fortune.'

The boys headed down the embankment with a spring in their step. First stop was the boat-house. Sam answered the door. Bobby handed over a packet of custard creams. 'These are from us. Happy New Year.'

Sam scratched his head and called for Eleanor. 'We have a present from the boys.'

Eleanor stood in the doorway. 'That's very kind of you. I'm glad you popped along. I hear Marcus has found himself a job at Archie's Alehouse. Please let him know he needs to join the Amateur Dramatics Society; we're short of leading men.'

The boys nodded and waved as they made their way back up the embankment to the Featherlow Forbes Menswear showroom. They pushed the door open and smiled at Charles. Billy produced the chocolate chip cookies from behind his back. 'These are for you from us. Happy New Year.' Tears welled in Charles's eyes, and he waved as the boys made a quick exit.

The twins ran back home before they forgot the message from Eleanor. Marcus was in the kitchen making a pot of tea. Bobby gave him the news. 'Eleanor says you need to join the theatre as she's always short of leading men.'

Billy pulled on Marcus's trouser leg. 'Can you put in a good word for us? It's been fun being in the panto. We can play any roles.'

Bridget called from the lounge. 'That video is on the television again. The one from Christmas Eve.'

Marcus and the children rushed into the room to

watch. The Newsreader's smile lit up the screen:

> *It's good to end the year with a heart-warming story. We were inundated with requests to show that video again. It's not every day Prince Charming delivers a baby and then goes on to rescue Cinderella from a freezing cold river. The village of Featherlow Bottom has brought joy to many this Christmas. Don't forget their Just Giving page. You can find the address at the bottom of this screen.*

*

Lady Featherlow was concocting another idea. She sat at the desk in her husband's study; the final night of the pantomime shouldn't go unnoticed. It's rare that Cinderella really does marry Prince Charming. There should be a party!

Annabelle closed her eyes and imagined how many chairs could fit into the Royal Box. She guessed there could be six at a squeeze. There were twenty spare seats in the front row of the Stalls. That meant several VIP guests could be invited to the final night. She'd draw up a draft list and run her idea by Eleanor.

*

Winston walked down the lane from the manor into the village. He felt ten years younger. He'd spent the last two days in London having his silver rattle valued and viewing some potential restaurant premises in the West End. Of course, Ellie would need to have the final say on the restaurant, but a few sites looked promising. When he reached the embankment, he bumped into Sam. 'Why, hello, Sam. Fancy a pint?'

Sam had been on his way to the tea room, but a pint on offer from Lord Featherlow was not to be missed. The men sat at a table in the bay window, and Archie walked over to take their order. Winston rubbed his hands together. 'Two pints, please, Archie. Any chance of a couple of portions of garlic bread too?'

Sam turned his nose up. 'Garlic bread? I can't think of anything worse. Pork scratchings are more my cup of tea.'

Winston chuckled. 'Trust me, Sam. You've not lived until you've feasted on garlic bread.'

The pints arrived, and Winston held up his glass to clink Sam's. 'Here's to the best Christmas we've ever had in Featherlow Bottom.'

Sam looked out of the corner of his eye at the garlic bread arriving. Archie placed it on the table; it looked a bit soggy but crispy at the same time. Lord Featherlow was tucking into his portion, so Sam decided to give it a go.

Winston wiped his mouth on a serviette. 'If *you* had

a silver rattle that had been given to one of your ancestors years ago by a King, would *you* sell it?'

Sam pushed the remaining bit of garlic bread into his mouth and chewed whilst thinking. He swallowed. 'That was delicious.'

Winston leant forward. 'Well, would you sell it?'

Sam wiped his mouth. 'Only if I needed to. What's at the bottom of this? Are you a bit short of money?'

Winston finished his pint and signalled to Archie for another round of drinks. 'Of course I'm not short of money. I do have a silver rattle though, that's been lost for years. It's now resurfaced and is worth more than anyone could ever imagine.'

Sam's eyes lit up. 'Well, if I were you, I'd have it insured, lock it away in a safe, and keep it for a rainy day.'

'What if there aren't any rainy days?'

Sam stared at Winston. 'Then you've been fortunate.'

Winston sighed. 'It doesn't seem fair that I have lots of money when there are people in this world who are struggling.'

Sam sipped his pint. 'I know what you mean. It sounds to me that you need to "do good" to "feel good".'

Winston stared at Sam. 'How can I "do good" without people thinking I'm looking down on them?'

Sam made a tongue in cheek suggestion: 'You could offer free holidays on your yacht to those in need. You could fiddle a raffle draw so that the neediest won the prize.'

Winston widened his eyes. 'Why didn't I think of that? You and Eleanor should go for a spin on the yacht with me too. You're a man of the seas. It's a bit lonely when I'm on there with just the staff for company. Annabelle's always too busy to take long holidays.'

Sam grinned. 'Invitation accepted! Now, what's happening about the Featherlow Bottom Benevolent Fund? They've been advertising it again on the News today.'

Winston rubbed his forehead. 'That's another worry. The Fund is going through the roof. We will, of course, give to the local hospice, but we need to think of something else worthwhile to support.'

Sam frowned. 'You do realise that the "local" hospice is over two hours away? When Olivia was in there, Charles made the round trip every day for six weeks.' Sam had a thought, and he decided to share it. 'Is there enough money to build one a bit nearer to here?'

Winston's eyes clouded over. 'Every day for six weeks?'

Sam nodded. 'He never missed one.'

Winston blew his nose. 'Did you know that Charles proposed after just three days of meeting Olivia? They married soon after that.'

Sam finished his pint. 'I certainly did. I always envied them. Over forty years married, they were. Eleanor didn't agree to live with me until we were in our twilight years, although I always carried a torch for her. Still, treading the boards in London was her big love. Long-distance relationships don't work. What with me at sea and her in the West End.'

Winston was now convinced he was doing the right thing to help Luke and Ellie. He also knew what he should do with the Featherlow Bottom Benevolent Fund.

23

A FINAL ENCORE

Lord and Lady Featherlow stood in the foyer of the Woodside Theatre greeting their guests. 'Thank you for coming at such short notice. Please help yourselves to canapés.'

Freddie arrived carrying a bouquet. 'Where would you like these?'

Winston gestured to the bar. 'Put them behind there for now.'

Sam and Charles arrived together. Annabelle went over to air kiss both of them. 'You two are in the Royal Box with our family. If you head off up there, a waiter will provide you with drinks and nibbles.'

*

Luke watched Ellie applying her makeup. 'I do so hope

this isn't the last time we'll be on the stage together.'

Ellie stood up. 'Will I do?'

Luke ran his eyes over the tattered dress that Cinderella wore in the first scene. 'You'll more than "do", Ellie Floris. I'm the luckiest man on earth.'

Ellie hugged her fiancé. 'I can't believe Lord Featherlow's sourced a restaurant already.'

Luke frowned. 'I thought there were a few possible sites.'

'Oh, I know which one is best. I used to work there. It's such a shame it shut down. I can just picture the signage: *Featherlow Floris Fine Dining* in green and gold.'

'What was it called before?'

Ellie lowered her eyes. 'Beau's Boutique Brasserie. The signage was in blue and grey.'

Luke's eyes widened. 'You can't work there.'

'Why not?'

'Won't it remind you of him?'

Ellie shrugged her shoulders. 'Yes. But in a good way. He fired me from there, and after I left, it closed down.'

Luke could see Ellie's point. Anyway, he'd been talking to Marcus earlier, and he had some news. 'Marcus is going to join the Amateur Dramatics Society here in the village.'

Ellie raised her eyebrows. 'Does he want to play leading man opposite Lucy? Won't Bridget mind?'

Luke chuckled. 'Lucy's done a runner and is now working in a fast-food restaurant in London. Rumour has it she's trying to get Beau Spinnaker lined up for the Manager's job.'

'What?! That's not possible. Beau's joining the family firm.'

Luke shook his head. 'Not any more. His father's cut the purse strings. Poor old Beau has to stand on his own two feet.'

Ellie frowned. 'Well, I must say I'm surprised about that. It's a good thing, though, that Lucy's left the village. There are lots of other women who could be leading ladies. They were too scared to come forward whilst she was still here.'

Luke's eyes twinkled. 'Bridget Baker will need to keep on her toes then. Marcus is a good catch.'

*

Sam and Charles were seated in the Royal Box when two little faces appeared around the door. Billy was most impressed. 'What are you doing in here? Are you famous?'

Bobby glanced longingly at the tray of canapés on a low table. Sam winked at Charles. 'Of course, we're famous. Didn't you know?'

Charles sipped his glass of champagne. 'We don't have any drinks we can offer you, but you can choose one canapé each before the other famous people arrive. I must admit we're looking forward to seeing you both perform on the stage. Make sure you wave.' The boys took a treat each and dashed out of the box.

*

The curtain rose to giggles from the audience. Lady Featherlow stared at her husband. 'What are they laughing at?'

As Ellie danced around the kitchen with a broom, Charles and Sam noticed why they were laughing. Billy and Bobby sat cross-legged underneath the kitchen table, waving up at the Royal Box. Charles gasped. 'I shouldn't have asked them to wave.'

Sam waved his arm high in the air. 'Wave back; then they'll go away.' Charles waved too. That worked; the boys crawled across the stage and disappeared into the wings. Sam reached for the champagne bottle and poured Charles another glass. 'I need one too after that; those boys are a handful. Goodness knows how

Eleanor's kept them in check for three weeks.'

Annabelle and Amelie were enthralled throughout the show. They couldn't take their eyes off Ellie, and when Luke burst onto the stage, they held their hands to their chests. You couldn't write a story like the one that had developed this Christmas. Who said romance was dead?

The sound of "Dancing Queen" was Winston's cue to go down to the stage. Annabelle whispered to him, 'Don't forget the flowers from behind the bar.' Winston nodded and headed off.

The final scene came to an end, and the curtain fell. The audience rose to its feet cheering and applauding until the curtain lifted and the cast appeared to take a bow. Winston stood in the wings next to Eleanor. 'When should I go on stage?'

Eleanor was beaming with both delight and relief. 'Oh, just wait a few minutes more until the applause dies down.' Eight minutes later, she gave Lord Featherlow a little nudge. 'Off you go.'

At the sight of Lord Featherlow, the audience stopped clapping and sat down. He smiled and waved to them before standing in front of a microphone. 'I would like to thank you all for coming here today for the final performance of Featherlow Bottom's annual pantomime. I also want to thank the cast.' Winston handed the bouquet to Ellie, and the audience clapped enthusiastically.

Winston could see Annabelle waving her left hand in the air and pointing to her wedding ring. Did he have to announce Luke and Ellie's engagement? He guessed his wife would be cross if he didn't. 'Oh, and I am delighted to reveal that Prince Charming and Cinderella are engaged to be married – not just for the pantomime but for real.' There were gasps and whistles from the audience, followed by a thunderous stamping of feet.

Now was the tricky bit. Winston had a few messages to get across. He looked down at the VIP guests in the front row of the Stalls, who were craning their necks to look up at him. Winston took a deep breath. This type of thing didn't come naturally to him. 'You will have seen from the television that this show has been one that keeps on giving. The general public may have laughed at our expense, but they've paid highly for the privilege. The Featherlow Bottom Benevolent Fund has reached a princely sum. It is with that in mind I took the time yesterday to visit Charles.' Winston gestured to the Royal Box, and Charles gave a small wave.

Winston continued, 'We have donated generously over the years to the nearest hospice, but that establishment is over two hours away from here. Now that we have the funds, it makes sense to source a suitable building closer to the village. When we have done so, we need to give it a name. I have agreed with Charles we will name it after his late wife, Olivia.' The audience rose to its feet and applauded wholeheartedly. Winston was relieved that part was over; he was more accustomed to speeches of the following kind.

'Whilst I have your attention here today, I would like to advise you of my next venture. I have decided to expand my business offering by opening a chain of restaurants. The first one will be in London, and my business partner is Ellie Floris.' There were gasps from the audience, and Winston continued, 'Not all of you know that Cinderella is a Michelin Star Chef. It will give us great pleasure to welcome you to Featherlow Floris Fine Dining when you visit the West End. What better way to enhance your theatre experience than to enjoy a meal before or after the show.' There were smiles and nods from the audience and another round of applause.

Winston continued whilst he was on a roll. 'Of course, we will need to keep the Featherlow Bottom Benevolent Fund topped up. With that in mind, I have decided to hold raffles so that those in need can win free holidays on my yacht.' Winston could see Sam shaking his head, and he quickly changed his wording. 'I mean for those in need of a holiday to get a chance to go on my yacht.'

Another standing ovation. This time the cheers and

whistles were aimed directly at Winston. He took a bow before looking at his watch. 'Now, I've rambled on a bit tonight, and I've only left five minutes for everyone to vacate the building. Please collect your possessions and congregate in the car park. I suggest you put on your coats.'

The audience gave one another funny looks. Lord Featherlow was such an eccentric sort. Still, the chance of winning a holiday on a yacht wasn't to be sniffed at – what a kind gesture.

Annabelle held onto Winston's arm as they stood in the crowded car park. Eleanor had rounded up all the children, and she stood in front of them. 'Are you ready, children? Start counting now.' There was a loud chant of: *Ten, nine, eight, seven, six, five, four, three, two one* . . . before the first firework lit up the sky.

Luke wrapped his arms around Ellie to shield her from the cold. 'I'll never forget this Christmas; it's been magical.'

Ellie held her left hand in the air, and her diamond ring sparkled under the colourful twinkling sky. 'I can't believe this is happening. Fairy-tales do come true.'

Marcus stood next to Bridget in the open doorway of her house, watching the fireworks light up the sky. 'I hope the boys are wearing their coats. Are you sure the baby won't wake up if we have the front door open?'

Bridget glanced up at him. 'No need to worry, the boys will be wearing their coats, and, by the way, the baby has a name.'

Marcus smiled at Bridget. 'She does? Let me guess. It must begin with a "B". Bonnie, Belinda, Beryl?'

Bridget blushed. 'She's called Marcia.'

Marcus's heart pounded, and he placed an arm around Bridget's shoulders. 'Marcia – I like that.' The couple watched the fireworks in silence – there was no need for words . . .

EPILOGUE

One Year Later

The snow had returned to Featherlow Bottom. It started falling on Christmas Eve, and by the morning of Christmas Day, the village was covered in crisp whiteness.

Lord Featherlow stood by his bedroom window, watching the robins feeding on a bird table. He took a deep breath and counted his blessings – life couldn't get much better than this. He could hear the sound of laughter coming from downstairs, and a smile lit up his face; Freddie, Amelie, and baby Freya had no doubt been up since the early hours. It was Freya's first Christmas, and Featherlow Manor was filled with excitement.

*

In the boat-house, Eleanor had made Sam's favourite breakfast; she only let him have it on special occasions. His eyes lit up at the sight of fried bread, white pudding, bacon, and eggs. He caught hold of Eleanor's hand before she darted away to check on the turkey.

'We had a great time in Monaco, didn't we? In all my years, I never guessed I would go there. Winston Featherlow has certainly come up trumps this year.'

Eleanor reached for her diary. 'You've just reminded me; I need to keep that week in July available. Where are we going again?'

'The Amalfi Coast.'

'Are you sure we should accept another free holiday?'

Sam took a sip of tea before answering. 'Winston said Annabelle is busy in July, so he's decided to go on holiday with a few friends.'

Eleanor felt honoured. "Friends" with the Featherlows, how did that happen? Still, it appeared to be the case. Eleanor and Sam had been invited, along with Charles, to the opening of Winston and Ellie's latest restaurant in March – Featherlow Floris Fine Dining was opening in Featherlow Bottom. The West End flagship restaurant was getting rave reviews; Henry Spinnaker was a regular there and recommended it highly to theatregoers in his magazine.

*

Charles had decided to spend Christmas Day on his own. The opening of Olivia's Cottage Hospice in October had been a monumental moment. Maybe next year he'd be ready to move on and take up an invitation to Christmas dinner. He'd already accepted Lord Featherlow's kind invitation to go on a cruise in July – he was quite looking forward to that.

*

Santa wasn't late this year at the Baker house. He'd arrived in the night whilst the children were asleep. Bridget was basting the turkey when Marcus received a text message. 'I've just heard from Luke and Ellie.'

Bridget wiped her hands on her apron. 'How are they getting on in Biarritz?'

'Ellie's not too keen on the skiing, but she's giving it a go.'

Bridget smiled. 'That's brave of her. I don't know that I'd want to go skiing on my honeymoon.'

'Where would you want to go on your honeymoon?'

'I've always wanted to go to Venice.'

Marcus rubbed his chin. 'I'd best go and check on the boys.'

Bridget had set the table and fed Marcia a fruit puree before Marcus returned to the kitchen with Billy and Bobby. Once the family were in the room, he closed the door and dashed upstairs.

The twins stood tall with their shoulders back, and Bridget wondered what was going on. The kitchen door soon opened to the sight of Marcus in his Prince Charming costume. Billy and Bobby went to stand either side of their mother before reciting: 'Cinderella, Prince Charming wants to marry you.'

Marcus bent down on one knee and held out a trilogy diamond ring. He'd chosen it especially for Bridget: three stones to represent past, present, and future. He looked up at her with his piercing silver-grey eyes. 'Marry me, Bridget, and I'll take you to Venice.'

Bridget threw a hand to her mouth; she was lost for words. Billy pulled on her arm. 'Just say "yes", Mum.'

Bobby untied his mother's apron. 'Take it off! Cinderella doesn't have an apron on when Prince Charming proposes.'

Billy begged to differ. 'Yes, she does!'

'No, she doesn't.'

'Yes, she does.'

The squabbling duo missed Bridget's answer, but they saw Marcus pushing the ring onto her finger, so they guessed they'd done their job well.

*

Back at Featherlow Manor, Winston was carving the turkey. The new chef had been briefed to surround it with holly. 'Oh my, oh my! What have I found here?'

Annabelle craned her neck to see her husband pick up a silver rattle from the serving platter. He walked over to Freya and shook it above the smiling baby in her Moses basket. 'I have a gift for you, my little sweetie-pie.' Winston placed the rattle in the basket, kissed his granddaughter's head and whispered, 'May each tinkle and chime bring a life that's sublime.'

Annabelle, Freddie, and Amelie sat open-mouthed as Lord Featherlow returned to take his place at the head of the table. Annabelle whispered to Amelie, 'He's started drinking too early again.' Winston winked at the photograph of his mother on the sideboard. He was surprised he'd remembered her words.

The doorbell rang, and Giles went to answer it. He returned with a bottle of claret, a bouquet of roses, a box of chocolates and a teddy bear. 'Charles just dropped these off for you all.'

Winston jumped up. 'Where is he now?'

'He's on his way back down the lane.'

Winston jogged to the front door; Charles was trudging through the snow in his wellies. Winston called to him, 'Charles! I need someone to partake in a glass of port with me, Freddie's not too keen on the stuff. You look like a port drinker.'

Charles turned around. 'Are you saying I have a red nose?'

Winston remembered another of his mother's sayings. 'Only Rudolf has a red nose, it's big and bright, and it truly glows.'

Charles let out a loud chuckle. 'It sounds like you've been on the port already.'

'Oh, come on, Charles. The turkey's going cold. Annabelle will be thrilled if you join us.'

Charles felt his loneliness begin to lift. 'Well, if you put it that way, how can I refuse?'

Winston called to Giles: 'Fetch Charles a pair of my slippers. He'll be joining us for Christmas.'

****

Printed in Dunstable, United Kingdom